Picking up her skirts, she ran across coarse European grass that pricked her feet. She skirted behind the fountain and held her breath.

Closing her eyes as she rested back against the cold stone, she knew what she ought to do when Raffa found her, and that was thank him for a wonderful evening and politely say good-night. But if she didn't want to take things to the next level, what was she doing here? And if Raffa didn't want the very same thing, why was he coming after her?

Every moment seemed to stretch into an hour, and she almost jumped out of her skin when he finally rounded the fountain. Even in the dark, she felt his black stare on her face. It scorched its way through her body, heating every erotic zone she possessed, but instead of yanking her into his arms as she'd halfway hoped, Raffa kept his distance. Had she misjudged this chemistry between them? Maybe she was in danger of making a fool of herself. Up-front as always, she went ahead to find out. "Kiss me," she whispered.

"That isn't sensible, Rose."

"I don't care," she replied stubbornly.

Welcome to the world of

The Acostas!

Passion, temptation and seduction!

Meet Argentina's most scandalous family! Follow these notorious heartbreakers' legacies in these other sizzling stories by *USA TODAY* bestselling author Susan Stephens:

All available now!

Susan Stephens

FORBIDDEN TO HER SPANISH BOSS

HARLEQUIN
PRESENTS

HARLEQUIN®
PRESENTS®

Recycling programs
for this product may
not exist in your area.

ISBN-13: 978-1-335-56804-5

Forbidden to Her Spanish Boss

Copyright © 2021 by Susan Stephens

This edition published by arrangement with Harlequin Books S.A.

For questions and comments about the quality of this book,
please contact us at CustomerService@Harlequin.com.

Harlequin Enterprises ULC
22 Adelaide St. West, 40th Floor
Toronto, Ontario M5H 4E3, Canada
www.Harlequin.com

Printed in U.S.A.

Susan Stephens was a professional singer before meeting her husband on the Mediterranean island of Malta. In true Harlequin style, they met on Monday, became engaged on Friday and married three months later. Susan enjoys entertaining, travel and going to the theater. To relax, she reads, cooks and plays the piano, and when she's had enough of relaxing, she throws herself off mountains on skis or gallops through the countryside singing loudly.

Books by Susan Stephens

Harlequin Presents

The Greek's Virgin Temptation
Snowbound with His Forbidden Innocent

Passion in Paradise

A Scandalous Midnight in Madrid
A Bride Fit for a Prince?

Secret Heirs of Billionaires

The Secret Kept from the Greek

The Acostas!

One Scandalous Christmas Eve
The Playboy Prince of Scandal

Visit the Author Profile page
at Harlequin.com for more titles.

For my reader friends across the world,
this is for you. Susan xx

CHAPTER ONE

A beachside wedding party on a private island
off the coast of Italy, owned by Raffa Acosta's
polo-playing friend Prince Cesar

'COME TO BED with me.'

Rose Kelly's jaw dropped. If it hadn't been a familiar voice that just husked in her ear, she'd have retorted with something unprintable. As it was, she swung around, ready to make light of it. 'Are you tired, *señor*?'

'Tired?' Her boss laughed and ramped up the infamous Acosta charm. 'Not even slightly. I decided to take pity on you, standing here, looking lost in the shadows.'

'Pity?'

Rose's defensive tone of voice made him look twice, but they were both off duty, and Raffa Acosta had broken his own golden rule first. 'Never fraternise with the employees' was rumoured to be branded on his buttocks, if tack-room gossip was to be believed.

'Joke?' he prompted with the worst attempt at looking penitent Rose had ever seen.

Was it, though? Raffa Acosta carried such a punch of testosterone, it was hard to believe anything he said in relation to the bedroom could in any way be regarded as a joke.

'I'm not lost, and there's no need to pity me. I'm just taking it all in,' she said with a sweeping gesture. 'The closest I usually get to this sort of thing is when I'm racing past the champagne tent to the pony lines during a polo match.'

'You're not missing anything, Rose.'

Rose took a fresh look at her boss. Raffa Acosta was enough to addle any woman's brains, but there was a new note in his voice. Accustomed to hearing him barking orders on his fabulous ranch in Spain—where, after three challenging, glorious years of proving that a five-foot-two Irishwoman could work the pants off any man, Rose was Head Groom in his polo stables—Raffa's confiding tone just now had surprised her. Was he as relieved as she was to be out of the post-wedding mayhem? When people had a few drinks, everything could change from decorously happy and polite to rowdy and increasingly wild. The wedding itself had been a fabulous occasion, but the pressure to chat and smile had been unrelenting.

His penetrating look raked her from head to toe. 'I didn't realise you and my sister were that close, until I saw you in the role of bridesmaid.'

'Oh, we've been good friends for some time.' Since

around nine o'clock that morning, but she wasn't going to drop Sofia Acosta in it by admitting Rose had been drafted in at the last minute to fill out a dress. Sofia always made time to chat to the grooms, and it had been a complete surprise, as well as an absolute pleasure, when Sofia had asked Rose to help her out on the morning of her wedding to Cesar. It was also a unique opportunity to experience the sort of high life a groom normally only witnessed from a distance. 'I hope you don't object to me being here.'

'Why should I?' Raffa queried, frowning.

Because she worked for him? And was supposed to be in the Prince's stables? Raffa had brought over a team of grooms to help with the horses he'd flown over to the island so the Prince and he could enjoy a few chukkas of polo. Rose had no right to be swanning around at anyone's wedding, and had switched around schedules to be here. If Sofia hadn't been so popular, she doubted that would have been possible. 'I'll make up the time,' she promised. 'And please don't worry about the ponies. I'd never leave them without organising proper cover for them first.'

'I don't doubt your reliability, Rose. Since the day you started work for me, you've been one of my most capable grooms.'

Capable? Coming from a sinful delight like Raffa Acosta, that was more a blow than a compliment. Shrugging it off, she concentrated on reassuring him. 'My colleagues have me on speed dial.' Producing a phone from the front of her dress, she flourished it in front of him, which, on reflection, was perhaps not the best idea. The bridesmaid's gown was skimpy, and Rose could be described as well built.

'I am reassured,' Raffa said, with a look that swerved her frontage, and landed squarely on her eyes. 'My sister couldn't have picked a better bridesmaid.'

'Well, thank you, kind sir.'

'Don't mention it.'

It was impossible not to laugh and relax when the great Raffa Acosta made a mock bow. He was a towering colossus of impossible good looks, with pheromones firing off the scale; it was growing harder by the second to remember that she worked for him, and her job meant everything to Rose. So much depended on her keeping it. Ponies had always been her life, and the money she earned went straight home to Ireland to pay for her father's keep.

'Best guess? My sister asked you to be a bridesmaid last minute.' Raffa's dark eyes burned into hers. 'Am I right? I'm thinking you took the place of the bridesmaid who breakfasted on sex and champagne—the woman who wasn't fit to be seen, according to my sister. I'd say Sofia got a lucky break, ending up with you.'

'As a sub,' Rose reminded him. 'I'm not a real guest. And, on that note—'

'Not so fast—'

Electricity streaked through her as she stared at his hand on her arm. 'People will talk.'

'Let them,' Raffa dismissed with a shrug.

'Don't you care that we're already attracting interest?'

'Do you?'

'No,' Rose admitted, 'but you should.'

'Why is that?' Loosening his grip, Raffa stood back.

'The god of polo getting off with his groom?' she said bluntly. 'How will that play in the society press?'

'I really don't care, and neither should you.'

'I'm only trying to protect you,' she protested.

One sweeping ebony brow lifted. 'Do I look as if I need protecting?'

'You look…'

Like every woman's dream lover—tall, dark and handsome, with more than a hint of danger about you. A gold hoop in your ear and that thick, unruly black hair, which, together with your deep tan and formidable build, makes you look more like a gladiator than a tech billionaire with a talent for playing polo.

'Well?' Raffa prompted.

'You look fine to me,' Rose teased with a one-shouldered shrug.

'Fine? Is that all you can find to say about me?'

'What more do you expect?' Rose frowned through a grin as Raffa's lips pressed down in the most attractive way.

'As we're clearly not going to bed, will you dance with me, Rose?'

The gladiator and the stable maid? That could work. If she could stretch her imagination for the span of a dance. Angling her chin, she stared up into his ridiculously handsome face. 'You really don't care what people think, do you?'

'Correct.'

The expression in her boss's eyes and the little tug at the corner of his mouth were all it took for heat to surge from Rose's toes to her belly with long stops in-between.

'The sun's going down,' Raffa observed, glorious eyes narrowed as he stared out to sea. 'We'd better dance, Cinderella, before you disappear.'

'Cinderella?' Rose queried with an ironic look.

Raffa held her gaze in a way that made everything riot inside her. Countering that feeling, she made up her mind and lifted her chin. 'Why not? Let's give them something to talk about.'

Rose led the way, but Raffa's hand was in the small of her back like an incendiary device for the senses. When they reached the dance floor, he dipped his head to murmur in her ear, 'There goes the bride and her new husband, so your duties are officially over. You've no excuse not to dance with me now, and, as I'm giving you the rest of the evening off, you're free to enjoy yourself any way you like.'

'Monopolise the chocolate fountain?' she suggested. 'Joke?' she added dryly in answer to Raffa's narrow-eyed stare.

'Okay, so you paid me back,' he conceded. Tilting his head, he regarded her in a way that made the heat in her body rush upwards to join the heat in her face. 'There's a lot of life left in this party,' he commented. 'Unless there's some other way you'd like to enjoy yourself?'

'Safely?' Rose suggested pointedly. 'Shall we dance?' Before this situation gets any trickier. 'Take care of my toes. I kicked off my shoes,' she warned. And then some devil got into her. 'I'd easily tower over you if I'd kept them on.'

Raffa laughed. 'Yeah, right. You'd still fit under my chin.'

The borrowed shoes had killed her, so Rose had ditched them as soon as she could, but now it felt as if she were about to launch herself into the arms of a giant. 'One dance only,' she stressed. 'If you can brave the curious and green-with-envy brigade, so can I.'

'Am I so popular?'

'I'm talking about me,' she shot back teasingly. 'Do you know how lucky you are, to be dancing with Rose Kelly, when everyone knows I prefer the company of horses?'

'I'm honoured you're making an exception, in that case.'

Raffa's second mock bow made everyone stop and stare. Rose hid her smile at the thought of the great Raffa Acosta dancing with Rose Kelly from a small farm in Killarney. The four Acosta brothers and their sister, Sofia, were known the world over for their brilliant minds, skill on horseback and the capacity for accumulating wealth, second to none. And here she was, flaunting herself with the best-looking brother. It seemed incredible. Maybe it was. 'Are you using me?' she asked suspiciously.

'For what?' Raffa demanded with a heart-stopping frown.

'To put off some annoying woman who's been chasing you.'

When he laughed, the blinding flash of strong white teeth only emphasised the depth of his tan. How gorgeous he was. A fact not lost on their fast-growing audience. 'If that's what you're up to, you could do better than me with my red hair and freckles. What about one of these sloe-eyed beauties over there, drooling over you?'

'Where?' He made as if to look around.

'I'm being serious,' she insisted. 'Or I'm trying to be, but you do make it hard.'

'Only because no one here compares to you.'

'You can take that tongue out of your cheek right now,' she scolded lightly.

'I'm being serious,' Raffa insisted with a perfectly straight face that threw her for a moment. It was one thing joking with the boss, and another when their stares met and held. 'Off-duty Rose has been a revelation to me,' he continued. 'You make me laugh.'

For the space of a dance, Rose thought, but as the banter continued she wondered if her boss was enjoying it as much as she was. Electric moments passed as they stood facing each other, waiting for the music to begin. Anticipating the touch of Raffa's hands on her body was almost as startling to Rose's senses as she was sure the real thing was going to be. At least, that was what she thought until they started dancing.

For a moment she couldn't think, breathe or exercise any of her faculties. It was a miracle her legs agreed to hold her up, let alone obey the rhythm that seemed to flow so effortlessly between them. Glancing around was another eye-opener. 'I was perfectly happy in the role of spear carrier, or place-filler, or whatever you want to call it, but I'm not so keen on every other woman at this party hating me.'

'I wouldn't trust you with a spear, and I certainly wouldn't call you a place-filler,' Raffa argued.

'What would you call me, then?'

'An entertainment.'

Was that bad or good? Look on the bright side. The women watching them had no cause to be jealous. Raffa couldn't have made it clearer that Rose's sole purpose was to lessen the tedium.

Was this really happening?

Rose didn't have a hand free to pinch herself as they danced on, as one was locked in Raffa's big fist, while the other was tentatively resting on what felt like a mountain of muscle. Grooms didn't get cosy with their employers, yet here she was, causing comment as she danced with Raffa Acosta, as if she belonged in his world.

Which she did, for tonight, at least, Rose reminded herself. Lifting her chin, she blocked out the jealous glances and silently dedicated this dance to all the wallflowers out there.

'Problem?' Raffa queried when she exhaled happily.

'Homesickness,' she lied. Admitting to the bliss of the moment would give him entirely the wrong idea, and she could always rely on the small farm in Ireland where she'd been born and grown up to make her feel wistful. Raffa's ranch was beyond fabulous, but there were times when Rose missed the old, ramshackle farmhouse, even with all its mixed-up history, cranky heating and creaking stairs.

'Are you sure?' he pressed when she frowned.

Those eyes could prise the truth from the Sphynx, but she could hardly tell him that along with wholesome dinners in front of a roaring fire, she was remembering her father drunk and her mother frightened he'd kill himself one day with the contents of a bottle. Dancing with Raffa Acosta was the most wonderful thing that had ever happened to Rose, but nothing would ever banish those memories.

'I'm sorry, I can't ease the homesickness for you, Rose.'

'I'll be fine in a minute.'

It might take several minutes. She wasn't used to caring comments, or tears stinging her eyes. She'd always had to be strong for her father. When her mother died, he'd gone to pieces, sinking ever deeper into an alcoholic haze. When he was sober, he mourned the wasted life he'd spent in a bottle, when Rose's mother had needed his support. Rose's father was a good man, a kind man, a gentle man, but he was weak. Sometimes Rose thought it was always the women who had to be the backbone of a family. They were the true warriors, the ones who never complained or gave up.

She would never give up on her father, and she would save enough money to find him a treatment.

Having given herself a stiff talking-to, she blocked out the past and smiled.

'I should thank you,' Raffa commented in response to the change in her manner.

She was surprised. 'For what?'

'For pricking my ego,' he explained. 'Why should I expect to have all your attention?'

'Because you're my boss? And you do have my attention. Ask any of the women here, and they'd say I'm lucky to be dancing with you.'

'That sounded dangerously like flattery to me.'

'And you get enough of that, I imagine?'

'Flattery is sweet food for those who can swallow it, but I'm more of a cheese and pickle man.'

Rose pinned a theatrical frown to her face. 'Are you saying I'm a navvy's wedge of a sandwich?'

When Raffa laughed she couldn't help noticing yet again that his teeth were perfect. He was perfect. It was dangerously easy to imagine that mouth and those lips creating havoc on her body. She shouldn't even be thinking like that, but nothing suited a man better than a sense of humour, in Rose's opinion.

'You're the only woman worth dancing with at this party,' he assured her as he twirled her around and around.

'Are you sure you're not just trying to make me dizzy?'

His answer was to yank her even closer.

There was a lot to be said for feeling light-headed. Raffa Acosta, who could have anyone he wanted, and capable Rose, who resembled one of those little dolls in an Irish gift shop, pleasantly plump and agreeably smiling, only short of wearing her red hair in plaits, dancing as if they belonged together.

'Tell me, why haven't we done this before tonight?' Raffa demanded. 'I had no idea what I was missing.'

'Honesty?' she suggested.

The smile on his face was something else to take away and store in her memory box. When they were working together on Raffa's ranch, he was all grim concentration.

'I didn't know what I was missing, either,' Rose confessed. 'I'd no idea you could loosen up to the point where you'd dance with a groom.'

'Don't tell anyone,' Raffa confided with a glance at all the avid faces watching them. 'Let this be our secret.'

'I promise not to say anything to tarnish your formidable reputation,' Rose pledged, enjoying the joke.

'You're lucky to have such an attractive accent, Rose Kelly, or I'd be forced to scold you severely for your cheek tonight.'

That could be nice.

No. No! She mustn't even think that way. This was one pity dance for the wallflower at a society wedding. Cinderella would soon lose her glad rags and don her work clothes to finish off mucking out the stables. But the music was upbeat, her heart was racing and Raffa didn't seem to care that they had become the biggest talking point of the night. 'Who has the accent?' she challenged, raising a mocking eyebrow.

'Are you daring to criticise my impeccable English accent, *señorita*?'

'No. I love the way you talk,' Rose admitted frankly. That sexy Spanish accent was the icing on an already delicious cake.

'Shall we dance on?' he suggested.

'Yes. Let's—but, there's something we need to get straight first.'

'What's that, Rose?'

'I won't sleep with you when the dancing stops.'

'I didn't have sleep in mind.'

'You're every bit as bad as they say you are,' she scolded, unable to help laughing out loud.

'Worse,' Raffa confirmed, with a look that scorched her from the inside out.

When the music finally stopped, neither of them seemed eager to part. Rose knew she had to make a move. 'Well, this has been wonderful, but I should be going—'

'If that's what you really want?'

'It is.' It was the last thing she wanted.

'Why am I not convinced?' Raffa murmured as he drew her into his arms.

Rose's heart pounded with a mix of excitement, at feeling Raffa's body so intimately pressed against hers. Tonight had turned out to be unexpectedly exciting, and reckless. That said, she didn't try to break free again. They were two people enjoying a party. What was wrong with that? Yes, they were causing gossip, but Raffa didn't seem concerned, and by tomorrow the gossipmongers would have something else to talk about. She was almost tempted to grab the mic to reassure the glitterati that Rose Kelly, without a penny to her name, let alone a title, would not hold Raffa's interest beyond tonight, because Rose was, as ever, determined to be herself, which left her with no place in Raffa Acosta's glamorous world. Whatever they said about Rose would be water off a duck's back, because she had no harsher judge than herself.

CHAPTER TWO

DANCING WITH THE most beautiful woman at a party was nothing new. Dancing with Rose Kelly was a revelation. He hadn't expected Rose to be dynamite off duty, or to feel so voluptuous in his arms. During his sister's wedding she'd unfurled like a flower, but it was the way Rose challenged him and made him smile that was the real surprise.

Alert as ever, she stared up at him. 'You seem distant. Is there a problem?'

'Beyond waiting for the band to start playing again?' He shook his head. 'No.'

That was a lie. Smiles had been in short supply since he'd witnessed the tragedy. Guilt had been his constant companion ever since. What was it about Rose that allowed him to hold the memory of his parents perishing in a plane crash and accept it as a scar surrounded by healthy tissue, rather than a wound that would never heal?

'Are you sure?' she pressed.

'I'm sure.' The concern in Rose's eyes threw him. He was the fixer, the one people looked to for answers.

And he didn't disappoint—except himself, one time, on one memorable occasion, when even his strong will had been incapable of preventing a tragedy.

'Okay, then.' She smiled faintly, obviously unconvinced.

Rose's luminous quality soothed his troubled mind, *and* attracted jealous glances, he noticed now. The urge to protect her was strong, but Rose was used to paddling her own canoe. She was the person people went to with their problems on his ranch. This was no milksop princess or society flitter-bug, but a strong, resourceful woman with a mind of her own. More than ever tonight, Rose had proved that appointing her Head Groom was one of the best decisions he'd ever made. 'I should apologise,' he found himself conceding.

'For what?' Her green eyes flared with interest.

'My shabby start with you this evening.'

Disentangling herself from his arms, she stood back, amusement dancing in her eyes. 'I've heard a lot worse. Six brothers,' she reminded him. 'And your charm won't work on me now. Nothing you say will persuade me to let you have your evil way with me. I've got too much to lose.'

'Your job?' he guessed.

'My self-respect,' she corrected him.

Tension crackled between them. Identikit women, boasting the same breasts, lips and overbleached hair, paled by comparison to an understated woman who could amuse him with nothing more than the thoughts that came out of her highly kissable mouth.

'Is it bedtime?' she teased, when a couple next to

them exchanged a meaningful look before leaving the dance floor.

'If I thought *you* were serious.'

She laughed. 'You wish.'

Rose's cheek was unparalleled, but she inflamed his desire. Feeling her body against his when they danced had proved that by some mysterious alchemy they fitted together perfectly. Lust tormented him.

But lust would have to wait. For the first time in his life, it seemed more important to get to know a woman. The cold hard facts provided by his team about each member of staff didn't come close to describing Rose Kelly, who was right in thinking they were causing a stir. He could practically read people's thoughts.

Who was this woman?

Where had she come from? Was she a close family member?

She must be, or why was she a bridesmaid?

He drew Rose to him on the thought that she was more than a hard-working employee. She was brave and tough, and tender too. The substitute bridesmaid standing in the shadows, keeping her thoughts to herself as she watched everyone else have a good time, was almost certainly a lot closer to the real Rose Kelly than Rose would have him suppose.

She was playing with fire, just by dancing with Raffa. The way her body was responding to his was ridiculous. She wanted him in a way that wasn't safe—not for her job, not for Rose. Had she forgotten the reputation of the unmarried Acosta brothers? Notorious for landing, conquering and moving on, they were hardly the safe option for a dance. Their sister, Sofia, was different. The seeds of friendship had been sown between the two of them that morning, when Sofia had confided in Rose that she was creating retreats for those who needed healing beyond the scope of conventional medicine, and Rose had immediately thought of her father.

'You're very quiet,' Raffa commented, so close to her ear that it tingled.

'Just thinking…'

'A dangerous recreation at the best of times. Good thoughts, or bad?'

'Mostly good,' she admitted, lifting her chin to meet the stare of a man who could easily muddle her thinking.

'You're not usually lost for words, Rose,' he prompted.

'I'll blame those six brothers again,' she admitted on a laugh. 'Bantering with them tends to hone your conversational skills.'

'Sofia would agree with you, I'm sure.'

'Then, you know what to expect from me,' she stated bluntly.

'Trouble?' Raffa proposed.

'As much as you want,' she offered wryly.

The hand in his was small, but strong, while the woman beneath the couture dress was as lovely as any here, but Rose had the edge in his eyes, because she was never afraid to speak her mind. His sister's friends were generally marked out by their manicured appearance, but, even on this most important of days, he could tell Rose's preparation had been rushed. He could imagine Rose devoting all her time to helping Sofia look perfect and doing little more than pelting in and out of the shower herself, leaving her womanly body smelling of soap. A mere slash of eyeshadow enhanced the emerald in her eyes, while the gloss on her lips begged to be devoured—

'Do you like the gown?'

'Do I…?' He laughed as she sucked in her stomach. 'You don't need to do that.'

'Oh, but I do,' she insisted. 'I was the closest to the original bridesmaid in build, but it's still a dress size too small for me. It's couture, you know.' She gave a twirl. 'And I was determined to get into it. I've never worn anything like it before. Talk about silk purse and sow's ear—'

'Don't you dare,' he warned. 'The gown looks lovely on you.' How could it not, when the silk and lace showcased a figure any woman would envy?

'Sofia said I can keep it,' Rose confided as they started dancing again. 'I feel bad, because I'll never have the chance to wear it again.'

'You don't know what life holds.'

This evening had made up his mind. He had a tour of business appointments coming up that required the use of his yacht, the *Pegasus*. It was the easiest way to move around Europe while entertaining in style. Rose would come with him. Her work in the stable was exemplary, leaving only one question: Could she handle the social aspect of the job?

There could be no hiding in the shadows on his

yacht. Rose hadn't held the post of Head Groom for very long, and it called for mixing with royalty and celebrity alike to discuss the merits of his various ponies. What better training ground could there be than a week on the *Pegasus*?

'It's time to go,' Rose announced as the band gave way to a DJ. 'I'll check on the ponies first, and then I'm off to bed. My own bed,' she stressed with a grin. 'We've got an early flight in the morning.'

'And if we didn't?'

'I'd still go to bed on my own.'

He couldn't help laughing. 'What about a drink first?' he suggested, reluctant to let her go. 'The ponies are safe, and you of all people know how important it is to remain hydrated.'

'Sensible me?' Rose suggested dryly, before cheekily adding, 'Or, capable me?'

'You got me,' he admitted wryly, hand to chest.

Not at all offended, she was laughing as they walked to the beachfront where a bar had been set up. A waiter quickly found them some seats.

'This is nice,' Rose murmured as she dabbled her feet in the water.

'You're a force to be reckoned with, Rose Kelly.'

'I'm glad you think so.'

'School, college, equestrian training—top of the class in every arena.'

Every arena except one. The romance she longed for had so far eluded Rose, and she doubted tonight would put that right. It was her own fault. She'd been too busy striving to be the best, to earn enough money to find her father some effective treatment, to spend time on relationships. 'Forged in steel and horse muck,' she agreed.

'And a great deal of hard work,' Raffa argued.

'Nice of you to say so…' Turning her face to the sky, she closed her eyes to drag deep on the scent of ozone, laced with the heady perfume of warm, clean man at her side. 'And now, look at me, reaping the benefits,' she teased, sitting up straight to smile into his eyes. 'Who'd have thought I'd find myself here?'

'You've earned this opportunity,' Raffa said firmly. 'Don't let anyone tell you any different. Your gift with horses is second to none, and you've got heart, Rose. The horses know it.'

But did he? She doubted it.

'You *have* been forged in steel, Rose Kelly,' he asserted. 'I've read your CV.'

'It was that, or crumble when my mother died. I'm sorry,' she jumped in, desperate to right the wrong. 'We've both suffered loss. I should have been more sensitive. Loss either breaks you or makes you, doesn't it?'

And now she'd made things worse. Raffa's stare was dark and long. Rose fell silent too. Everything had been upbeat until she'd taken them both to a place of grief. She knew little about the death of his parents apart from what she'd read in the press, that the plane crash had affected all the Acostas, even Sofia, who'd been very young at the time. Whatever Raffa's torment, she couldn't leave him in that dark place on his own.

'I'm sorry for your loss.' As she spoke, she impulsively covered his hand with hers.

'As I am for yours, Rose,' he murmured, pulling his hand away.

'I still have my father,' she said lightly to cover her embarrassment. 'Just.'

'Just?' Raffa queried, dipping his head to interrogate her with one of his penetrating black stares. 'Is there something I don't know that I can help you with?'

'No. Nothing.' *Everything.* But she wouldn't ask Raffa for help. What would he think of her? Didn't everyone go to him for some sort of assistance—usually financial? This was Rose's family problem, and she would sort it out. By herself.

Seeing Raffa still brooding, she went in with a distraction. 'Tomorrow, this magic will all be over. You'll be back to riding the pants off the competition and running your billion-dollar corporations, while I'll be mucking out your horses.'

He laughed, but not before she'd seen the well of grief behind his eyes—grief that mirrored her own. 'If you ever want to talk?' she couldn't help adding.

He stiffened. 'I'm not in the habit of discussing personal matters.'

That response should have been enough for Rose to keep her mouth shut, but she'd never been good at that. 'Why not? Talking helps. Why is talking about you off limits?'

'I'm your boss?' Raffa suggested with a look that warned Rose again to back off.

'Thanks for reminding me.' She also silently thanked

six argumentative brothers for prepping her well for this type of combat. 'For a moment there, I thought we were two human beings sharing experiences on an equal footing.'

She held her breath, uncertain as to how Raffa would respond. And had to stop herself exclaiming with relief when the same humour that had attracted her when he'd come out with such an outrageous opening statement to her at the wedding crept back into his eyes. 'What if I told you your boss is considering your next training programme, to advance your career?'

Rose's heart leapt out of her chest—or felt as if it had. Each module she'd embarked on so far at Raffa's prompting had been equivalent to an advanced course in equine care. The thought of another thrilled her to the bone—but not to the point where she wouldn't be honest with him. 'I'd still tell you the truth.'

'That's what I hoped you'd say.'

Rose's head was spinning. She loved her job. All good things sprang from it. Her career was not just the bedrock of Rose's self-belief, but the means by which she hoped one day to pay for her father's treatment. On those rare occasions when he was sober, and she saw the man he could be, Rose redoubled her determination to live up to the pledge she'd made to her mother to take care of the family. Any advancement in her career would help her to do that.

'I'll see you receive the details as soon as possible,' Raffa was saying.

'I'd appreciate that.'

'Goodnight, Rose.'

Dismissed, she stood, recognising that tomorrow was already here. Reality had been stalking them, and the magic was now well and truly gone.

'Goodnight, Señor Acosta. And thank you once again for everything.'

He sat in the same chair for almost an hour after Rose had left. The moon beamed down like a spotlight on the ocean, while he turned a spotlight on himself. He'd never opened up to anyone. Not even by the smallest hint had he revealed the wounds Rose had uncovered with her words. To protect his brothers, and most especially his sister, Sofia, he avoided talking about the past in case he intruded on their grief. So why tonight, when accompanied by this young woman who worked for him, with whom he'd enjoyed some low-level flirting, had he been prompted to lay bare a part of himself that was as raw today as the day he had stood watching in helpless horror as his parents' plane crashed in flames on the runway in front of him?

Impatient to be thinking about the past, when there was nothing to be done about it, he sprang up. He'd seen the sadness in Rose's eyes and had done something about it. Workwise, she was a worthy candidate for advancement, and he'd give her every chance.

In other ways?

There were no other ways where Rose was concerned. He'd seen how emotional involvement led to disaster. If he'd diverted that plane—insisted his parents travel on a regular flight, rather than taking their small private jet with a drunken pilot at the controls—they could still be alive today.

The pain that thought brought him was warning enough to keep his feelings in check. He was a man of business, a man of polo, a man who…

Would never have a family of his own?

He braced his shoulders against the truth. The man who, on his last polo tour, had looked at his brothers and Acosta cousins with envy, as they'd played with their children and laughed with their partners. Good luck to them! They'd been lucky. He had more sense than to tempt fate to smile on him where love, luck and family were concerned.

Having thanked the wedding organisers for giving his sister a wonderful day, he headed back to the palace. He never went to bed without checking on the ponies first. The grooms travelling with him were more than capable of doing this, but there was always the possibility that they might need something, or one of the horses had refused to settle. The fact that Rose could be carrying out the same checks was irrelevant to him, except that nagging part of him that insisted they weren't done yet—and not just in the professional sense.

When he reached the palace stables the grooms were changing shifts. One sleek, spotless, air-conditioned interior of a top-class polo stable was much like another, and Prince Cesar's facility made him long for home. In that, he and Rose weren't so dissimilar, he reflected as he entered the security code to gain entry.

Rose might enjoy her job, but he suspected that part of her heart would always be in Ireland.

Once inside the stable block, he shed his jacket and rolled up his sleeves.

'Raffa!'

'Lurking in the shadows again?' he reprimanded, though Rose's voice had caressed his senses like a welcome embrace.

'Working, not lurking,' she assured him.

Rose was smiling when he walked up to her, holding an armful of kittens. She'd changed out of her gown into an old pair of jeans and a shapeless top, with a pair of serviceable muckers on her feet. 'You call that work?' he challenged.

'Tell that to the kittens,' she said as she buried her face in soft fur.

Work lights illuminated her face, making Rose appear more radiant than ever.

'Do you want to hold one?'

He declined. 'Better put them back with their mother. She'll be missing them.'

'You're right,' Rose agreed reluctantly. 'I found them in one of the stalls, making a break for freedom.'

Animals were a great leveller, and a great indicator of character too. 'You don't have to make up your time for attending the wedding by working late,' he made clear as they went to find the mother cat's nest.

'You're here,' Rose pointed out. When he didn't reply, she added, 'And while you're here, I should ask—did I go too far with the cheek tonight?'

He raised a brow. 'Just put the kittens back in their nest.'

Rose seemed reluctant to part with them, and turned to give him an imploring glance. 'If you even hint at the fact that rescuing kittens has been the best part of your night, I will take offence,' he warned.

He received an amused glance. 'I'm sure you won't stop teasing me any time soon,' Rose declared. 'So, yes, if you must know, the best part of tonight was dancing with you.'

Her frankness disarmed him. 'But you're more comfortable with animals?' he guessed.

'It would be rude to admit that.'

'But it's true?' he pressed.

'They're not as dangerous as some of the humans I've met,' she admitted.

'I hope you don't count me amongst those threats?'

'You'd better be one of the good guys, or I'm in trouble,' Rose countered, humour brightening her eyes. 'Although you certainly don't look like one of the good guys to me.'

'To prove my credentials, I'll escort you to the door of the grooms' quarters.'

'That's very good of you, but it doesn't prove a thing,' she pointed out. 'Do I have cause to worry?'

'Not tonight.'

'Well, that's honest enough. You have my permission to walk me to the door—but no further.'

'Thank you, *señorita*,' he mocked lightly. 'I'm hugely honoured to end my evening with such a crushing blow to my ego.'

'You'll get over it,' Rose assured him.

The verbal banter between them was entertaining, but reality had landed with a bump, Rose mused with a twist of her lips. Cinderella would quite literally be returning to her garret at the top of a palace tower, while he would spend the night in supreme luxury in one of the Prince's best suites. 'After you,' he invited.

As Raffa politely gestured she should go ahead of him, Rose tried to squeeze past, but the mother cat had made her nest in a narrow passage where space was extremely limited. This made it inevitable that they brushed against each other. Instead of apologising and moving on, which was what she should have done, she paused and stared up at him. In that moment, she could have sworn Raffa wanted to kiss her.

He didn't kiss her.

It was amazing what the body could drive the mind to believe. 'Excuse me,' she said politely.

'Of course.' He took a step back.

Not that it wasn't a joy to move past him and feel those hard muscles resisting the press of her softly yielding body, but that would be the only thing yielding tonight. She'd do nothing to risk the advancement of her career, because there was so much at stake— not just Rose's career, but her father's future hung in the balance too.

CHAPTER THREE

LONGING WASN'T so much a state of mind as a real physical ache, Rose concluded as Raffa, true to his word, escorted her back to the grooms' quarters. Of course she wanted him. Her body demanded she sleep with him, but too much hung on keeping her job.

She'd settle for a lifetime of wondering *What if?* because that was far safer. Hadn't she seen an excess of emotion taking her parents on a roller-coaster ride, with far too many downs and not nearly enough ups? When emotion was in the mix it wasn't just sparks that flew, but whisky bottles and teacups, and anything else that came to hand.

When they reached the old oak door that marked the entrance to the grooms' quarters, she held out her hand to shake his. 'Thank you for a wonderful evening.'

'Thank *you*, Rose. I've enjoyed myself immensely.'

The touch of Raffa's hand was shockingly arousing, and she had to quite literally remind herself to let him go. 'Have a great night's sleep—'

'You're not turning me down again, are you?' Raffa teased.

'That I am,' she confirmed.

* * *

Who was this woman to keep him up all night? With a disbelieving shake of his head, he stood beneath an ice-cold shower the following morning, wondering why the freezing water was having no effect. It wasn't subduing his interest in Rose—his body was straining at the leash.

Once he'd prised her from the shadows, Rose Kelly had proved more intriguing than he could possibly have expected. Even Rose's cold shoulder was the hottest thing to have happened to him in quite a while. Her lilting Irish accent and those sparkling emerald eyes, combined with her quick wit, and a body to die for, might have seemed a cliché if anyone but Rose had been involved, but he knew she was the genuine article.

She'd bewitched him, he concluded as he towelled down roughly. No woman should be allowed to do that. Hadn't he made a pledge not to draw anyone close? Yanking on his jeans, he pulled on the first top that came to hand. It wasn't just the fact they were flying home this morning that made him eager to start the day, but the thought of working alongside Rose that drove him on. Raking impatient fingers through his still damp hair, he left the room, slamming the door behind him.

And then he got a call.

Preparing the ponies for their flight was one of Rose's favourite jobs, but she couldn't help listening out for Raffa. Where was he?

As soon as she finished work, she went to the tack room to grab a glass of water before the flight, to find a new notice pinned up on the board.

Señor Acosta regrets leaving before thanking the grooms for their hard work during this trip.

Raffa had left without saying goodbye? So much for enjoying himself last night! Thank goodness she'd had the good sense to go to her own bed alone, instead of inviting him to join her. Imagine how she'd feel if she had slept with him.

Worse than now? Was that even possible?

Now she noticed something glinting on the floor. Swooping down, she recognised the sparkling black stone encased in white metal as one of the cufflinks Raffa had been wearing last night while they were dancing. Later in the stable, he'd been in shirtsleeves, she recalled.

The find was not a glass slipper, and Rose was no Cinderella, but she'd have to get it back to him somehow. Tucking it safely inside the breast pocket of her shirt, she returned to work.

'Rose, have you seen this? It's addressed to you.' Rose's friend and fellow groom Adena excitedly handed over a note. 'How was the wedding?' Adena asked with a grin.

'Spectacular,' Rose admitted.

'I thought as much,' Adena said. 'Looks like a letter from the boss,' she added, leaning over Rose's shoulder.

So, he hadn't forgotten her. Ripping the envelope open, Rose found an invitation to spend the following week on Raffa's yacht! *Incredible. Exciting. Terrifying.* Then reality hit. This was no romantic billet-doux, but a call to action by her boss. She read it again.

> *I have to know you're confident enough to handle all the responsibilities of Head Groom, including entertaining royalty.*

For a moment Rose was panic-stricken. Royalty? Could she even curtsey? She couldn't do it—not a chance!

Why not? Hadn't she made the successful transition from a small farm in Ireland to Raffa's fabulous facility in the heart of Spain? Surviving six brothers meant she was no shrinking violet, and a working life was all about exploring possibilities. So long as entertaining royalty didn't involve feathers or veils, she was up for it.

'On board his yacht,' Rose murmured thoughtfully.

'He uses the *Pegasus* as a floating office and entertainment centre,' Adena explained.

'I see,' Rose murmured, wishing she had more experience to draw on. It wasn't her ability to adapt to these new demands that concerned her, but her naivete where men were concerned. Flirting at the wedding was one thing, but being enclosed on a yacht for a week with a man she found so devastatingly attractive…six brothers looking over her shoulder and a drunken father in the background hadn't exactly given Rose much chance to learn about men.

She'd done okay so far, Rose reasoned. She'd just have to rise to the occasion, and hope Raffa didn't do the same.

Landing by helicopter on a swaying deck in the dark was quite an experience. There was no sign of Raffa in the welcoming committee, which consisted of two uniformed stewards who had obviously expected Rose to arrive with a great deal of luggage.

Shouldering her backpack, she smiled her thanks as a man who introduced himself as the purser helped her down. To say the ground was shifting beneath her feet was an understatement, but she was determined to make the most of this new adventure.

Try telling yourself that when you can't get a signal on your phone, or your balance on the deck! Clinging to the rail, she smiled brightly at the purser as he waited patiently for Rose to follow him. This was the experience of a lifetime, she reminded herself, not a trial by ordeal.

Once they were inside the spectacular interior of the mammoth yacht, Rose began to relax, though another shock was waiting when the purser showed her into her quarters. She had expected something small and cramped in the bowels of the ship, but he had just opened a pair of grand double doors on the most amazing suite of rooms.

'All for me?' She breathed like a muppet as she took in what looked more like an upscale penthouse than a cabin on a ship.

'Yes, ma'am,' the purser replied. 'All for you.'

Two very different worlds had just collided. She

knew horses could often cross the boundaries of race, wealth and class, and Rose had always been comfortable working alongside Raffa on his ranch, but here she felt…completely at sea?

'I hope you'll be comfortable,' the purser said as he showed her around the most sumptuous accommodation imaginable.

'Are you sure this is where I'm supposed to be staying?'

'If you'd prefer another suite—'

That wasn't what she'd meant at all. 'This is absolutely perfect.' If entirely over the top for a groom. Alarm bells started ringing when she stared at the emperor-sized bed.

'You'll find the dressing room is stocked with most things you'll need,' the purser continued, 'but if there's anything else you can think of that's missing, we can have it flown in by helicopter.'

Of course they could, Rose marvelled. 'Well, this is wonderful.' And miraculous. How did they even know her size?

Leading her through to a dressing room with the dimensions of a conventional lounge, the purser opened drawers and cupboards on an array of high-end goods.

'Sorry to repeat myself,' Rose said, frowning, 'but are you sure all this is for me?'

'Señorita Adena was asked to fill out a list of things you might like.'

Adena? Ah, that solved the mystery, but why hadn't Raffa asked Rose straight out? Didn't he trust her to ask for the right things to fit with his lifestyle on board the yacht?

The thrill of looking around made Raffa's presumption fade away. Not only had Adena proved to be the best of friends, she'd done the most excellent job.

'You'll find a letter detailing plans for each day,' the purser informed Rose. 'In your free time, you may use the swimming pool on the sun deck, where you can call for drinks and snacks. Please enjoy the rest of your day.'

'You're very kind.' She had to force herself to walk slowly to the door as she showed him out, but the moment the door had closed behind him she rushed back to pounce on the letter. Ripping the envelope open, she pulled out a note. Embossed with the logo of a flying horse, it said in Raffa's bold black script:

You will be dining in the open-air salon tonight at eight o'clock. Dress: casual.

Casual, as in banged-up jeans and an old faded top? She doubted it. Shower first, with the suit she normally wore for interviews hanging in the bathroom to steam out the creases. A fresh blouse later, and she'd be ready for whatever lay ahead.

The temptation to take a quick tour of the outfits in her dressing room proved irresistible. It would be rude not to. Adena had gone to so much trouble. These were clothes Rose had only seen in magazines before. Caution was not a word she would use in connection with them. Glamour was the watchword here.

'I miss you, Adena,' Rose murmured as she stared in awe. 'And I promise to wear at least one of these fabulous gowns, if only as a nightdress...'

Rose reckoned a swim before dinner might relax her. The way she felt—excited, aroused and bewildered at the thought of seeing Raffa again in these extraordinary surroundings—threatened to take her mind off the reason she was here. Plus, she had to brace herself for disappointment when he treated her not as a dance partner, or a woman he wanted to spend time with, but as his head groom—which should have been enough for her, but really wasn't. Selecting her armour, she chose a bright green swimming costume with matching cover-up. This was no time for blending into the shadows.

A sense of urgency pervaded his work the moment Raffa learned Rose was on board. Finishing the last of his video calls early, he found it impossible to concentrate on anything else until he'd seen her. A head groom gained unique insight into his life, meaning the position called for the utmost discretion, along with encyclopaedic knowledge about horses, together with the ability to communicate that knowledge to all types of people. This week would prove whether Rose was ideally suited in the long term for the job.

She was certainly suited for his bed, he reflected before he could stop himself as he pulled on his swimming shorts. The purser had informed him that Rose was in her stateroom, so he planned to swim and clear his head before meeting up with her. Having spent the morning behind a desk, he was eager for exercise.

He arrived at the pool to find Rose had settled in before him. The surprise of seeing her there was a punch to his senses. With her back to him, and a large-brimmed hat hiding her spectacular hair, it was clear she'd gone for impact, rather than discretion, by choosing an emerald green swimsuit that outlined her spectacular figure. A matching cover-up was draped across the chair, but she made no attempt to reach for it as she turned to face him.

Rose.

Grabbing a swim towel from the stack on the side, he slung it around his neck.

Removing her hat, Rose placed it carefully on the sunbed at her side. With a graceful action, she reached up to free her glorious hair from the colourful scarf containing it. As she raked her fingers through the waist-length tumble, the effect it created was, to Raffa's mind, a fiery cloud to compete with any sunset.

'Raffa!'

'I'm sorry if I startled you.'

She clutched her chest. 'It's good to see you,' she said. 'Thank you for inviting me to your yacht. Not as a guest, of course,' she added quickly, as if wanting to reassure him on that point.

'I hope my purser has made you comfortable?'

'If I had to walk the plank anywhere, I guess this is the best place to do it.'

He raised a brow. 'Let's hope that won't be necessary.'

His body urgently demanded one thing, while his mind demanded another. He required the best of the best in the role of Head Groom. Rose was that individual. There'd be other women he could have in his bed.

But they wouldn't be Rose.

'The *Pegasus* effortlessly covers vast distances, allowing me to entertain at short notice. No hotel can compete with the facilities here.'

'I heartily confirm that,' Rose agreed.

Something had to give. How could she be so cool when the wolf inside him was howling with impatience? 'Swim?' he suggested curtly, willing his body to behave.

'Why not?' Rose replied eagerly.

'You do swim?'

'I do,' she confirmed, with what he thought was a glint of amusement.

Rose accepted the invitation gladly. Having seen Raffa in black swimming shorts that revealed more than they concealed, she badly needed cooling off. Her senses were in free fall, but wanting him was dangerous to both her heart and mind. How to stop wanting him was the problem. Raffa was her boss. Rose was here to prove she could handle all aspects of the job. Expanding her working life was an exciting prospect, and one she embraced with enthusiasm…but there was nothing to stop her having a little harmless fun along the way.

The water was deliciously cold against her overheated skin. Rising to the surface, she drew in air before slicing through the water as if racing her brothers.

Within moments a form appeared beneath her. It was Raffa, swimming underwater on his back. She kicked even harder, but, the wretch he was, he pulled ahead.

'You cheated,' she accused when they reached the far end, by which time she was laughing with sheer pleasure.

'I cheated by swimming underwater?' Raffa queried with a frown. 'You should have set the rules before we began. You're a great swimmer. Fast,' he approved.

'Six brothers, remember.' She spoke with the broadest of smiles, appreciating her brothers more in that moment than she ever had before.

'And a competitive spirit,' Raffa added. 'You'll need that to go far in your career.'

'I won't disappoint,' she promised fiercely, loving the way they could switch from play to work and back again.

'This experience will be good for you, Rose. You don't know how strong you are until you're tested.'

'Prophetic words?' she queried as Raffa placed his big hands on the side of the pool and sprang out. 'Not up for a race, then?' she shouted after him.

Stopping dead in his tracks, he turned. 'Is that a challenge, *señorita*?'

'*You* mentioned competitive spirit,' she reminded him.

The wait of a few short seconds felt endless to Rose, and then Raffa turned slowly to face her. 'Race me?' he queried.

'Why not? I race my brothers.'

'Head start?' he offered.

'If you think you need it.' Without waiting for a reply, she launched herself backwards in the water. Raffa followed and, in a stroke or two, overtook her.

'You should have mentioned you swam for Ireland,' he teased when they reached the far side.

'Good race,' Rose gasped.

When Raffa sprang out, he dipped down again to take hold of her hand.

'Thank you,' she said as he hauled her out of the pool as if she weighed nothing.

'You're an excellent swimmer,' he remarked as he tossed a towel in her direction.

'And you're an excellent liar. You beat me by half a pool's length.'

'Only because I was going slowly,' Raffa teased, with a look that heated her from the inside out.

'I'm challenging you to a rematch,' she shouted after him.

'I look forward to it.'

'So long as you don't allow the result of that swim-off to affect your judgement when it comes to my job?'

'I enjoy swimming with you,' he said, displaying the power in his formidable torso as he opened his arms wide. 'We can have that race any time you like.'

'I'll take you up on that,' Rose promised.

He grinned.

'This is a fabulous way to spend your time,' she remarked as they settled down on the sunbeds.

'It is a great way to travel,' Raffa agreed. 'Efficient,' he concluded with a thoughtful nod.

An incredulous laugh burst out of her. 'Only a billion-aire could say that. The rest of us catch the bus, or hope it doesn't rain when we take the bike out of the shed.'

She was never quite sure how far she could push it, and it was a relief when Raffa laughed too.

Seeing his life through Rose's eyes was like seeing it through a new and extraordinary prism. As he followed her gaze across the pristine deck, he noticed, for per-haps the first time, what she meant. Their surroundings were spectacular. And so was she. Unaffected by wealth or status, Rose was one of those truly rare things: a very nice person. And as such, he should give her a swerve. There was too much darkness inside him, too much unresolved anger and grief. Bad things happened to people he cared about, and it would be ridiculously easy to become involved with such an intriguing and attractive woman.

Was Rose so different beneath the surface? Didn't she have shadows too?

He wouldn't add to them. 'Dinner's at eight o'clock sharp,' he reminded her.

'Don't worry, I'll be there.'

He held her stare a dangerous beat too long, before springing up and walking away. 'I have business calls to make,' he called over his shoulder.

'And I have swotting up to do, in case you feel like testing me this evening on the names of all those peo-ple you want me to meet.'

'Later,' he confirmed.

* * *

She watched Raffa disappear down the companion-way and had to resist the urge to chase after him, but that would be entirely unprofessional and, thankfully, sensible Rose knew it.

Back in her own suite, she took a shower then tugged on jeans and a top before sitting down at the desk to glance over the notes she'd made. She was usually a fast study, but that was before Raffa invaded her mind.

I must not screw this up.

The words banged about in her head. It would soon be eight o'clock, but the touch of Raffa's hand on hers when he'd helped her out of the pool with a grip so firm and sure and safe… And with that look in his eyes that had been the complete opposite of safe. She must not screw this up, indeed!

The next problem was not what to wear. The contents of Rose's luxurious dressing room might be tempting, but temptation was the last thing she needed tonight. Securing her hair in a sensible ponytail at the nape of her neck, she considered doing without make-up. After all, what was make-up but cheese in a mousetrap, when the look she should be aiming for was dry biscuit? But Adena had worked so hard to make sure Rose lacked for nothing. It would be churlish to throw those efforts back in her friend's face. Adena would be hungry to hear about everything…including the high-end products still in their cellophane wrappers.

A flick of mascara, and some nude lipstick later, and Rose was ready to meet her fate.

Glancing at her phone out of habit, she grimaced and shut the door again. The press was still discussing the mystery woman seen dancing with 'The World's Most Eligible Bachelor' at his sister's wedding. Gossip had already identified the woman as none other than Rose Kelly, a groom from Ireland who worked in Raffa Acosta's stable. 'The deadly Acosta charm works its magic again.'

'Not on me,' Rose pledged out loud, but she couldn't resist reading on.

'Yet another willing victim sacrificing herself on the altar of lust. And who could blame her?' the journalist asked archly.

Rose wasn't given to cursing. She heard enough of that language at home, but tonight she made an exception. Had Raffa read this too? Were these few column inches in the press all that her hard work added up to? It was naive to think she could keep the encounter with Raffa at the wedding a secret when everyone with a phone was an amateur paparazzo, but to suggest she'd jump into bed with a man simply because he was sex on two hard-muscled legs was…

Not going to happen, Rose determined as she smoothed the skirt of her serviceable suit.

Worse luck.

CHAPTER FOUR

IF SHE'D BEEN worried about Raffa's reaction when he read the articles about them in the press, it was nothing to Rose's reaction when she saw where she was about to eat supper. The scene on deck was like something from a film set. She couldn't help exclaiming, 'Do you eat like this every night?'

Raffa swung around, and so did her heart. In fact, it lurched in each and every direction at once, and it took all she'd got to bring it back, to adopt a friendly but serious expression as she walked towards him.

'Good evening, Rose.' Pulling away from the rail where he'd been lounging, Raffa advanced with a steady, purposeful step.

'I didn't expect this,' she admitted with a long glance at the dining table. Dressed with crystal and silver beneath a gently rippling white canopy, the area was lit by flickering candles, which suggested a lot more than a business dinner.

'You thought we'd eat burgers, and hang with a couple of beers?' Raffa suggested dryly, before explaining, 'My chef wanted to test some of the recipes for my champagne reception—'

Rose's heart jumped alarmingly once again. She'd somehow managed to park the socialising element of the week in an underused part of her mind. Not that she didn't party in Ireland, but a ceilidh down the village hall would hardly compare with a celebration on board the *Pegasus*.

'—so I told the chef this would be the ideal occasion,' Raffa continued smoothly.

'Of course,' Rose agreed. 'Who are we receiving? At the champagne reception, I mean.'

Raffa had already turned away to speak to the steward. 'No champagne, thank you. I'll call if we need anything more. His Serene Highness, for one,' he said, switching back to Rose. 'Don't look so worried. My champagne reception is nothing compared to the Prince's annual charity ball the following night.'

'And when is the champagne reception?' Rose asked.

'Tomorrow night.'

'As soon as that?' Rose's throat dried. 'You'll be busy.'

'And so will you,' Raffa assured her. 'There won't be a better opportunity to launch you into society. You haven't been long in the job, and these events will give me the chance to introduce you around and see how well, or not, you're received.'

As the World's Most Eligible Bachelor thief, Rose didn't imagine she'd be welcomed with open arms.

'Aren't you pleased?' Raffa prompted.

Rose reminded herself that this was El Lobo, the Wolf, as Raffa's black stare stabbed into hers. 'It all sounds very exciting,' she lied, doubting six great hulking brothers had prepared her for the type of high-society individuals she would meet on Raffa's superyacht. 'I'm looking forward to it enormously.'

'Is that why you've lost your appetite?'

Raffa missed nothing. Laden platters had been placed in front of them, and Rose couldn't face a thing. 'It all looks delicious.' Her stomach grumbled right on cue. When had she last had something to eat?

Finally, she ate, and the food was indeed delicious. She told Raffa so in a series of appreciative moans. She could do this. She had to do this if she wanted to progress in her career. When he began to talk about the ponies they both loved, she knew it would be possible, because this was once again the serious-minded man she worked for and respected, the man whose unparalleled equine knowledge had drawn Rose to work for him in the first place. It wasn't long before her enthusiasm for the topic spilled over, and the glamorous occasions ahead of her lost their power to intimidate.

Rose continued to impress him over dinner. The press had been less than kind to her since the wedding, suggesting she was an opportunistic gold digger, making the most of her surprise inclusion in his sister's wedding. He was accustomed to being picked over by the press, but it was new for Rose, yet she made no mention of it. Even when he broached the subject, she brushed it aside, and got back to talking about the animals she loved.

'Rest easy, where those articles are concerned,' he said as she continued to weave the magic of unaffected charm over him. 'They won't influence my thinking on your work. The post of Head Groom is too vital for that.'

'Thank you for the reassurance,' Rose said as she dabbed at her mouth with a napkin. His gaze followed her movements. The evening had grown chilly while they'd been eating, and when she reached for the throw on the back of her chair, he leaned forward and draped it around her shoulders.

'I've learned so much while I've been working for you,' she admitted, staring up at him with the frankness in her eyes that made her irresistible. 'I adore my work, and I'm open to any and all developments where my career is concerned. I've got such wonderful colleagues. We wouldn't be the team we are without them, and I've made so many friends.'

As she talked, he saw the passion in her eyes, and suddenly wanted that same passion directed at him, but relationships outside his immediate family had proved impossible since the tragedy. He could go so far and no further, before his concern to protect others from his darkness kicked in. So many things had become impossible on the night he saw his parents perish in front of him. His mother used to say love is beautiful, but he thought it agonisingly cruel.

Something in his thoughts must have communicated to Rose and triggered a surprising response in her. 'Tears?' he queried. 'Does your job mean so much to you?'

'It means everything to me,' Rose confessed fiercely, pulling herself together fast. 'When my mother fell ill, she made me promise to take her place and look after the family. My brothers have flown the nest, but my father's still a constant worry, so I have to succeed, to be in a position to support him, just as my mother asked.'

Hostage for life, he thought, realising that Rose would never believe she'd done enough. He was glad she'd confided in him. It explained the shadows in her eyes, and her constant drive to be the best. He could relate to those emotions.

'Everything I do is geared to keeping the family afloat,' she continued. 'And please don't feel sorry for me. Remember, I chose this path.'

Had she, or had Rose's direction in life come from a desire to break free from what must have been a difficult childhood? 'Thank you for your company tonight,' he said formally, bringing the evening to a close. 'You've got a big day ahead of you tomorrow, so try to get some sleep.'

Rose stood and thanked the stewards, who reappeared at exactly the right moment to hold her chair and open doors. 'Goodnight, Raffa. Sleep well.'

He doubted that would happen with Rose lying in a bed only a few yards away from his.

Rose was determined to keep things upbeat the next morning at breakfast. She and Raffa had trodden a tightrope over grief the previous evening that could alter the course of this week, if she dwelled on it. Working in a top stable was tough for all concerned, which meant a good-humoured, purposeful attitude was essential.

'Good morning,' she said brightly, joining Raffa at the table. The only problem now was Raffa in cut-off jeans, revealing rock-hard muscles in his deeply tanned legs, and a top that showed off everything, including his infamous wolf tattoo.

But this was not the time for feasting on Raffa, who launched straight in with the news that he had more conference calls to make that morning. 'Meanwhile, you will liaise with the galley staff and everyone else on board the *Pegasus*, to ensure the champagne reception runs smoothly tonight. I have some additions to the list of people I've asked you to talk to at the event. It always helps to have a plan.' His black stare lingered on her face, unreadable and inconveniently arousing. 'Rose?'

'Sorry.' Moistening her lips, she quickly refocused. 'I'm delighted to help in any way I can. I'm so looking forward to meeting your guests.'

'No careless revelation of trade secrets,' he warned.

'You can rely on me for discretion.'

'We'll heave to in the ocean off the coast of Monte Carlo. My crew has entertained like this many times before, but I'm looking to you to add something more…an extra dimension, if you will.'

'Of course.' Excitement gripped Rose as she

switched on the part of her brain that delighted in organising the heck out of things.

Raffa went on to explain that the *Pegasus* would be dressed for the reception as well. 'Pennants, lights, champagne, music, and, of course, you'll join me in welcoming His Serene Highness on board.'

'Of course,' she agreed, imagination running riot at the thought of sharing the occasion with Raffa.

'The event starts at eight. Things move fast in the Acosta world,' Raffa cautioned.

'I think I already know that,' she pointed out good-humouredly, 'and I promise not to let you down.'

'Excellent,' Raffa said briskly. 'The following night, as I mentioned to you yesterday, I will be the Prince's guest of honour at his most important charity event of the year. There'll be more people for you to meet at the ball, so I suggest you mug up on the names I've given you.'

To hear the brazen invitation to sin sitting next to her coolly detailing plans for upcoming events made Rose want to smile at the unlikely clash of sex and heat and business.

'It's an opportunity to start building relationships at the very highest level,' Raffa explained, staring straight into her eyes. 'You'll be adding to your knowledge of how deals are done in the horse world. Your reputation in Ireland was second to none, and now you're going global, Rose.'

'I'm excited,' she admitted, and not just by the professional opportunities Raffa was putting her way. 'I'm guessing formal dress will be required?'

'Just bring your quick wits along,' he advised, lounging back in his chair.

'I will,' she vowed, eager to make a start on her homework for the night.

Trepidation successfully quelled, Rose was bouncing off the ceiling with anticipation in her dressing room later that same afternoon at the thought of the night ahead. A champagne reception *and* a prince. Thank goodness Adena had arranged for such an amazing selection of fabulous gowns for Rose to choose from. Slipping into the green silk sheath she'd selected for the event, she gasped at the transformation in the mirror. She looked so elegant she could almost believe she belonged in Raffa's very different world.

The phone rang, distracting her. It was Raffa wanting to know Rose had checked up on everything she was supposed to.

'You sound breathless,' he remarked. 'Are you sure everything's all right?'

Learning to walk in high heels with a skirt that wrapped around her like a mummy's bandage wasn't the easiest thing she'd ever had to do. 'Perfect,' she lied, steadying herself on a handy table as she kicked off the perilous heels.

'You can't be tense tonight,' Raffa warned. 'My guests will sense it, and they won't relax if you don't, which means no one will have a good time. Did you find something you're happy to wear? If not, I can always arrange for the helicopter to take you to Monte Carlo to select something else.'

If that didn't knock the air out of her chest, nothing would. 'That won't be necessary,' she managed with studied calm. 'Thank you for the offer, but there's more than enough choice here—'

Rose stared at the receiver in her hand as the line cut. What would Raffa think when he saw her in this? Was it too much? She smoothed her hand down the sleek silk clinging to her body like a second skin. No reaction from Raffa would be a slap in the face, while even the smallest reaction might steal her attention from the only thing that mattered tonight, which was promoting Rancho Raffa Acosta. No place-filler tonight, she would instead be co-hosting a party with a billionaire. And yes, it would be nice to have Raffa look at her with something more than speculation in his eyes, but there could be no loitering in the shadows this time. It would be full-on guest-hosting from the get-go.

Hair down, make-up on, and a spritz of scent later, she was ready to embark on the next stage of what she was coming to think of as Rose's Remarkable Journey.

Glamorous evening? Bring it on.

Dressed overall, and with all lights blazing, the *Pegasus* looked fabulous tonight. Rose stood in awe for a moment in the entrance to the grand salon, the main reception area on the yacht, staring past all the trimmings to where one man stood alone on the deck. She didn't need hand holding, which was just as well, as Raffa's life was one long line of business discussions, so he'd doubtless have his own itinerary for tonight.

The *Pegasus* wasn't so much a billionaire's folly as a floating necessity that allowed him to move his office around the world. No wonder he was such a polo fanatic. Playing the game was the only downtime this titan of the business world allowed himself.

She stopped in her tracks, hearing the first of the tenders approaching. Moments later the chatter of excited partygoers floated across the water. Changing direction, she prepared to greet the first of their guests.

It was accepted etiquette that everyone must be in place before the Prince arrived, and Rose was gripped by the same excitement as the rest at the thought of a royal visitor, but even that paled in comparison to watching Raffa circulate amongst his guests. He eclipsed everything and everyone around him. As distinguished as a prince, he was as sexy as humanly possible, having dressed for the occasion in an immaculately tailored white jacket and slim-fitting black trousers. With midnight blue sapphires flashing at the cuffs of his crisp white shirt, he was hot and hard, and heading her way. Fumbling in her evening purse, she cursed softly, only now remembering his missing cufflink was in another bag. *Next time!* She'd get it back to him tomorrow latest.

'I see you found a dress,' he commented.

Did that slight angling of his chin, and that look in his eyes, denote approval? 'I did,' she confirmed.

'Great choice of gown,' he said with the lift of a brow.

Sound faded as they stared at each other, until all she was aware of was Raffa. 'I'm glad you approve.'

His lips slanted, as if to let her know that, whatever he thought of the dress, he knew she'd have worn it anyway. 'You've also done a good job with the details.'

The flowers in her hair, or the addition of bite-sized canapés to accompany the flutes of champagne?

'The guests you'll meet tonight know how to enjoy themselves,' Raffa informed her. 'You'll find the party achieves a momentum of its own.'

Like so many things, Rose thought, basking in awareness as Raffa placed a hand in the small of her back to guide her across the deck to the first of the people he'd like her to meet. This turned out to be a prominent professor at the forefront of animal therapy, and he and Rose were soon deep in conversation. She thanked Raffa silently with a warm glance. 'You're welcome,' he murmured before moving away.

When Raffa returned, Rose and the professor were still talking animatedly. 'You'll have to excuse us, Professor,' he apologised. 'The Prince's helicopter is due to land, and we must be there to greet him.'

'Of course…' The professor bowed over Rose's hand. 'I hope we have the chance to talk again very soon.'

'You seem to have made a good impression there,' Raffa remarked as they made their way to the helipad. 'I'm glad. The professor's important to me. He saved me at a time when I had so much anger inside me, it threatened to consume me. He made me see that animals could help to soothe the human spirit.'

'They have an innate healing quality I've always been interested in pursuing,' Rose confessed.

She could guess when Raffa had been at his lowest point, and was glad the professor had been able to help him. She only had to think back to how her own emotions had run the gamut after her mother's death, from despair to hollow emptiness, and on to anger at the injustice of random fate, to understand the turmoil that so often accompanied grief. This was the most insight Raffa had given her, but now was not the time to draw him out even further. He'd tell her more when he was ready to—or, not at all.

He felt a jab of something unexpected as he watched the Prince talking to Rose. Had he ever experienced jealousy before? The Prince was charming, and Rose was easily the most attractive and interesting woman at the party, but she was no Cinderella, waiting for a prince to sweep her off her feet. She was a hardworking woman, who knew her job, and whose natural charm and ability to listen and be genuinely interested put everyone at ease. When the Prince moved away, Raffa watched Rose work the crowd with all the flair of an accomplished host. She made everyone feel special, and had quickly become the hub around which his party flowed. His one complaint was that the food had turned from savoury to sweet by the time she returned to his side.

'You've arrived just in time to gorge on chocolate,' he said as a steward offered them a plate full of sin.

Rose laughed. 'Don't tempt me.'

'Dive in—one for each hand,' he advised.

She glanced at him and blushed. 'I'd love to, but

I'm guessing our guests won't appreciate a chocolate handshake—'

'Allow me…' Selecting a delicious-looking treat from the tray, he touched it to her lips.

Rose's gaze flashed up and darkened, almost as if he'd made a move to kiss her. The temptation to do so overwhelmed him, especially when her tongue crept out to lick her lips, but she turned in response to the chatter of their guests, and quickly excused herself to introduce some newcomers around. That was what he wanted, of course. A successful party depended on the swift reactions of the host.

It should be what he wanted, he amended, as Rose charmed yet another group. She was careful not to leave anyone out—except him, apparently. With an amused huff, he pushed away from the rail and set out to work the other side of the deck.

Guests took precedence over anything else. Even Raffa, though her gaze kept straying to him. He could turn on the charm at parties, but Rose had glimpsed the darker side of their glamorous host. It would be good for both of them to let some light into the darkness, but Rose had never had the time to properly deal with the past, and guessed Raffa was in a similar position. Maybe one day they would manage it, but, with the party in full flow, tonight was not the right occasion. She had stewards to help and food to bring out, as well as what seemed like a constant stream of misplaced items to find for various guests.

When the evening finally drew to a close, and the

Prince thanked them both for a most wonderful party, Raffa was quick with his praise. 'You worked hard tonight,' he told her as they stood watching His Serene Highness's helicopter lift off the deck. 'Thank you, Rose.'

'Thank you for the opportunity,' she replied with genuine warmth. 'It's been a wonderful evening. I didn't expect to enjoy it quite so much.'

'You were the hit of the night,' he reassured her, 'and you've another big day ahead of you tomorrow, so you'd better get a good night's sleep.'

'I will,' she assured him.

They stood facing each other, Raffa with his head dipped in Rose's direction. Something in his eyes made Rose raise her chin. There was a moment, a very long moment, when she was absolutely certain Raffa would kiss her this time, and Rose was equally sure she'd kiss him back.

Seconds ticked by, and when—once again—nothing happened, oddly disappointed, she turned to go. 'You get a good night's sleep too,' she called to Raffa over her shoulder.

Thoughts of Rose plagued him throughout the night. Reliving the moment when the thought of kissing her had crossed his mind and taken hold made an ice-cold shower a necessity.

The ice-cold shower was no help at all. Lifting his face to the spray, he attempted to banish lustful thoughts from his mind.

That went well.

Cursing viciously, he cut off the stream of water, stepped out and grabbed a towel to dry off. This was why he never allowed himself to feel. Feelings only got in the way. Sex had been his saviour in so many ways. It brought physical relief and blanked out the emotional pain of the past for however long it lasted. Planting clenched fists on the marble surface of the washstand, he stared at his reflection in the mirror. A hard man stared back. Rose Kelly had no place in his mind. He had nothing to offer her, apart from employment opportunities on his ranch.

Raking his hair with stiff, angry fingers, he grimaced as memories of the past came flooding back. When he'd discovered the pilot had been drunk, he'd cursed himself for not boarding the private jet to check it out himself before it took off with his parents on board. He'd learned a vital lesson that night. Love was not invincible. It could be destroyed by something as simple as a bottle of whisky in the wrong hands.

Impatient at this lapse back into a past he couldn't change, he scowled and left the bathroom. Rose's soothing balm was what he needed—her laughter, her challenges and an enlivening dose of her cheek. Admittedly these were all a poor substitute for sex, but something had to help him relax.

Only, seeing Rose in person would have to wait. Business meetings were stacked up in front of him, and it was the charity ball tonight. Texting Rose, he reminded her of her itinerary. There must be no slackening off from the standard she'd set last night.

I have meetings all day. You have hairdresser, beautician, etc. at noon. Report to the helipad eight p.m. sharp. R

He thought about adding a few encouraging words, but Rose had done very well without them so far.

Rose was still rubbing sleep from her eyes when her phone pinged. 'I should have put it on silent,' she muttered, squinting to read the short note. Seeing it was from Raffa, she sat bolt upright, instantly awake. Touching her lips, all she could think about was their almost kiss. Was Raffa thinking about her, and remembering it too?

Heart in her mouth, Rose scanned the text fast. And frowned. Clearly not. No mention at all of last night, just a list of appointments she was expected to attend. Crushed, she was in no mood to comply. Hairdresser? Beautician? What was she—a show pony? Then a worse thought occurred: Had she made a fool of herself last night—misjudged the look with that gown? No. Even in such a glamorous frock, she'd been dressed down in comparison to some of the women.

Sitting cross-legged on the bed, she pulled faces at her reflection in the wall mirror. She scrubbed up as well as the next person. It wasn't as if she were planning to attend the ball in her pyjamas. Hairdresser? Hadn't she been doing her own hair all her life? As for needing a beautician? You couldn't correct a face full of freckles without a bucketful of Polyfilla, and no one was coming near enough to slap on a face full of that. And what exactly did 'etc' mean? A stylist perhaps? That could be useful, Rose concluded with a frown. She could do with someone to teach her how to walk in high heels.

Raffa would apparently be busy until he attended the ball, but at least that spared her the usual interrogation over breakfast this morning. He was not an easy taskmaster. She had studied hard at equestrian college, but Raffa had obviously eaten and fully digested the texts. There wasn't a thing he didn't know about horses.

Not seeing him wasn't all good. Apart from the obvious basking in the glow of a flame that burned so bright, the lack of Raffa meant losing her anchor in this sea of plenty, and there was no guarantee he'd be her rock tonight. Raffa would be seated with the Prince, while Rose would be so far away, she'd probably be sitting out in the yard.

A flutter of apprehension gripped Rose, until she reminded herself that she'd managed pretty well last night, and would manage again. The one thing she'd never had a problem with was standing on her own two feet, and any expansion in her duties signalled a welcome progression in her career.

A knock on the door jolted her out of the reverie. Was it Raffa? He'd look great carrying a breakfast tray. She smoothed her hair. 'Come in…'

It was a uniformed steward with a smiling explanation. 'Señor Acosta thought you might like breakfast in bed today.'

With Raffa, yes, Bad Rose suggested. 'That's very

kind of you,' Good Rose said politely, lapping up the sight of a tray laid so perfectly it was fit for the Ritz.

'Your beautician and hairdresser arrive at noon,' the steward said, as if he'd been asked to reinforce Raffa's message. 'Señor Acosta suggests you relax for the rest of this morning.'

Suggests? Unless Rose was mistaken, that was an instruction. Raffa wanted her to be fresh tonight, and out of his way today. Had that 'almost kiss' affected him too—in a way that made him determined to stay away from her—or was she making too much of it?

'Breakfast looks delicious,' she called tactfully after the steward as he left the room, though her appetite had all but disappeared.

Releasing her death grip on the butter knife, she started to prepare herself mentally for the palace ball. The first thing—the most vital thing of all—was to finally remember to return Raffa's cufflink. She couldn't entrust it to anyone else.

Searching out the evening bag she intended to use that night, she secured the black jewel in the small zip-up pocket. Her next task was to remind herself how much she enjoyed meeting new people, and how she relished diverse topics of conversation. What was so different about tonight? A ball at the royal palace would be daunting for anyone, though for Raffa it would be all about business. Networking was a crucial part of his life. And now, for some annoying reason, a parade of unfeasibly beautiful females, all with the world's most eligible bachelor in their sights, plonked itself in her mind. She tried reassuring herself that her only task was to choose a dress to wear, while those imaginary women, in competition for Raffa, would be at it tooth and claw.

Closing her eyes on that unfortunate image was no use at all, for there they were, taunting her as they sashayed up and down behind her eyelids.

Where the choice of gown for tonight was concerned, glamour the heck out of it was the only answer.

CHAPTER FIVE

His TRANSFER FROM ship to shore was seamless, but he couldn't relax until he knew his team had arrived at the palace. Until he knew Rose had arrived at the palace. Infuriating woman! Why was she always in his head? No matter how many times he told himself that caring for anyone outside his immediate family might attract fate to take an interest, he appeared unable to stifle his concern for Rose. The evening would be dull without her. Even if she appeared in her interview suit she would light up the room.

He'd gone ahead of his team to meet the Prince in private to discuss some upcoming polo matches, and now he was pacing the ballroom like a youth on his first date.

Where the hell was she?

Glancing at his watch, he spat out a curse. It was only two minutes since the last time he'd looked. He had skipped a reception after his business with the Prince to make sure he was here in time to reassure Rose that this vast space, with its ceiling painted by some protégée of Michelangelo, glorious marble floor, stately pillars and glittering chandeliers, was merely top dressing for what really mattered, which were the charities that would benefit from the after-dinner auction tonight. He was confident the stuffed shirts present would be captivated by Rose's warmth and charm, and he couldn't wait for them to meet her. What a surprise they'd have, in the form of a spirited Irishwoman with laughter in her eyes and kindness in her heart.

Kindness was perhaps Rose's greatest asset, he reflected, that and her voluptuous body, which was outstanding. His thoughts jumped to what she'd wear for such a dazzling occasion. It was impossible to predict anything where Rose was concerned, apart from the fact that she'd be true to herself, and that in itself set her apart.

Spying His Serene Highness making directly for him forced him to concentrate on the here and now. There could be no more glancing up the sweeping marble staircase to see if Rose had arrived, or staring at his watch, willing the hands to move, but he found it hard to concentrate on what the Prince was saying, and could only trust he dipped his head and nodded in all the right places as the Prince went on. 'I'd like to discuss the details of our polo matches with your head groom present—'

A flurry at the top of the stairs distracted them both. They weren't alone in inhaling sharply. The palace ballroom had hosted many beautiful women, but none could compare to the woman at the top of the stairs.

Rose had paused in a halo of light, to take in her surroundings and get her bearings, he guessed. The impulse to leave the Prince, mount the stairs and escort her down the sweeping staircase was overwhelming, but this was Rose. This was her moment. No hiding in the shadows tonight, she was obviously determined to put on a good show for him, and if that meant dressing like a queen, and lifting her chin to warm the room with her smile, then that was exactly what she would do.

'I have to say, you have impeccable taste,' the Prince observed in a discreet murmur.

'Rose is an exceptional horsewoman,' he replied, refusing to besmirch Rose's reputation with even the slightest hint of impropriety.

As he had expected, Rose didn't wait for anyone to escort her down the steps. Several contenders tried, and were all charmingly but firmly dismissed. Chin up, eyes smiling, Rose appeared to float down the stairs wearing the highest of heels. How long before she kicked them off? he wondered with amusement.

Leaving the Prince with a gracious bow, he waited at the foot of the stairs. Rose's exquisite green eyes smiled into his, but the enchantment of her presence was infectious, and the Prince lost no time in joining him to welcome Rose.

'You'll sit with us on the top table,' His Serene Highness insisted with his customary charm.

'I'd be honoured, Your Serene Highness,' Rose replied engagingly.

Only the swift blush that pinked her cheeks told him how surprised she was to receive this invitation. When she glanced at Raffa and raised an awestruck brow, he smiled and nodded with genuine pleasure for Rose.

'You look stunning,' he whispered when the Prince left them to join his wife. He recognised the peach-coloured dress with its illusion underskirt as one he had particularly favoured. The close fit did more than hint at the perfection of the body underneath, while the colour brought out the highlights of gold and copper in Rose's ravishingly beautiful hair. She had chosen to wear her hair down tonight and looked amazing.

'Stunning?' she queried in the same discreet tone. 'You mean, I'm not wearing breeches smeared in mud?'

'I mean,' he said, 'you look beautiful tonight.'

'You're blinded by the jewels I'm wearing,' she teased, referring to the spectacular diamond earrings and necklace he'd had couriered to the *Pegasus* especially for tonight. Everyone was clearly wearing their best pieces, and he hadn't wanted Rose to feel left out. 'I wondered what *etc* meant when I read your text,' she added with an impish smile, 'and now I know.'

'I'm pleased you chose to wear them,' he admitted as he escorted her to the Prince's table. 'I was by no means certain that you would.'

'I couldn't leave them rusting away in that old jewel case. I'll never get the chance to wear things like this again,' she added, touching her fingertips reverently to the intricate diamond necklace. 'So, I thought, why not?'

'Why not, indeed?' he agreed, enjoying the novelty of a woman who would never take such extravagant jewels for granted. 'Enjoy them while you can.'

'There is another possibility,' she suggested.

Her words made him tense. Was Rose about to disappoint him like all the rest by being so overcome by the obvious value of the jewels, she'd see no further than his bank balance? 'What's that?' he queried mildly.

'I agree to become your mistress,' she said, perfectly straight-faced. 'Then, I can wear jewels like this all the time.'

Disappointment slapped him in the face, to the point where he almost missed what she said next.

'Even when I'm mucking out,' she added with a grin. 'In fact, I'd like to order a tiara to complete the set. As Head Groom, I should have some sort of badge of authority, don't you think...?'

There was a moment of stunned silence and then he laughed as such a strong sense of relief flooded through him. He'd certainly met his match in Rose. 'I think that's an excellent idea—'

'Hold on!' She held up her hand. 'I've thought of an even better one.'

'What's that?'

'You donate the jewels to the charity auction tonight.'

'Donate the jewels?' he exclaimed with surprise. 'I had intended for you to keep them—to wear on occasions like this.'

Rose gasped, hand to chest. 'What a responsibility! Where would I keep them—in the hay store? Look, I don't mean to be ungrateful, but there are some fabulous fakes out there at a fraction of the cost, if you think it's important for me to wear jewels. Personally, I just can't see why they're necessary. Either people are interested in what I have to say about your ponies, or they're not. And, just think about it,' she confided, bringing her fragrant head close to his, 'the proceeds from the sale of these gems could be put to far better use.'

He shrugged. 'You make a good argument. Auction them, by all means. I'm only sorry I didn't think of it myself.'

'That's what a head groom's for,' she teased.

'Do you take anything seriously?' he asked as Rose's eyes fired with an engaging triumph that had nothing to do with her going one better than him, and everything to do with Rose's generous nature finding an outlet tonight in the charity auction.

'Oh, yes,' she told him with a level stare. 'I take my job very seriously indeed.'

'Which is exactly why I brought you here.'

'Then I'd better get to work,' she said, breaking the spell.

Their lips had been close, stares locked, as the fate of the jewels was decided.

Feelings he'd ruthlessly subdued for years continued to bombard him as he stepped back. 'The Prince is already seated. We should join him.'

'Is that you hinting I've said enough?' Rose asked with a twinkle.

'More than enough,' he confirmed mock-sternly as he took the greatest pleasure in escorting Rose to the Prince's table. Lavishing extravagant gifts on a woman had always been his way of easing his guilt at feeling nothing for them, but Rose needed no such gifts or grand gestures. She thought with her heart when it came to riches, and had touched him deeply with her suggestion to auction the jewels.

'You look happy,' she remarked as they approached the Prince's table.

'I am,' he admitted. Rose made him look outwards, instead of brooding on the past. How could he not feel happy about that?

Dinner, as expected, was excellent, and it was further enhanced by Rose, who once again played her part to perfection, charming everyone. When the plates were cleared the auction began. There were some big-ticket items, attracting huge sums of money, but when Rose was introduced, and stood to offer her stunning jewels for the charity, there was a collective gasp. The Prince, who had already been informed of the donation, had invited Raffa to take the rostrum, to handle what was confidently expected to be a record-breaking sale.

The first bid was a million, and it went on from there. At one point, Raffa jokingly reminded his audience that Rose was not part of the deal. She smiled sweetly at him, to a chorus of groans, but it was the look that passed between them that briefly stilled the crowd. The magic of a supposed liaison between them had the added bonus of driving bids even higher.

'Congratulations!' The Prince stood to applaud them both as Rose's jewels were sold for an astonishing amount. 'You make a great double act,' he remarked. 'Thank you both for your most generous donation.'

Rose handled the praise with her customary modesty, and soon had the Prince laughing at some quip she'd made. Later, when His Serene Highness had left the table, she reached across to hand Raffa something. 'What's this?' he asked. Instinct drove him to close his fist around Rose's pale, cool fingers.

'If you let go of me,' she whispered discreetly, 'you'll find out.'

'And if I don't?'

'You'll have one cufflink, instead of a pair. You dropped it at the wedding, when we were in the stable.'

Shock and a bittersweet sense of relief shot through him with the force of an arrow. 'And you've waited until now to give it to me?'

'Thank you is enough,' she scolded him lightly.

'Thank you,' he gritted out ungraciously.

Making his excuses to their table companions, he pushed back his chair and stood, indicating that Rose should do the same. For once, she complied, almost certainly because his face was so thunderous and she feared a scene.

'What have I done wrong?' she demanded as he ushered her at speed in the direction of the French windows leading on to the palace gardens. He stopped short on the veranda at the top of the steps. Losing the cufflink had devastated him, but his carelessness wasn't Rose's fault and he shouldn't take his self-recrimination out on her.

'You kept it safe for me all this time,' he confirmed gruffly.

'Of course I did.' Rose looked at him with concern. 'I didn't realise it meant so much to you, or I'd have made sure to get it back to you right away.'

'You kept it as a talisman instead.'

'Yes…it did feel like one,' she admitted with a puzzled frown. 'You think that too?'

'The cufflinks are special. I've always believed they carry a special magic. I've been kicking myself for being so careless ever since one disappeared.' Holding the jewel tightly in his fist for a moment, before stowing it safely in an inside pocket, he explained, 'They were the last gift from my mother.'

'Oh, Raffa…'

Rose was right. There were no words. After a silence, she led the way down the steps. His uncertain mood must have left her wondering if he'd follow, but as always Rose was both undaunted and sensitive to what was needed most, which was distance between them and everyone else at the Prince's ball.

She carried on through the subtly lit gardens, without attempting to speak, or comfort him. She didn't need to. An understanding had sprung between them, based on their shared grief.

How Rose wished she could reach inside Raffa and drag out all his pain. She felt so frustrated as they walked along. A determined woman didn't like to admit defeat, nor find it easy to accept there was a problem she couldn't solve, but so much of Raffa remained hidden. The only way forward, Rose decided, was to look at the small part of his grief he had shared with her as the first step on a long journey. Would she be a part of the rest of that journey? There was no way to tell. They'd be returning to the ranch soon, where life would return to normal. Rose would be fully occupied in the stable, while Raffa resumed his busy life. Their sole connection would be work, with chances to be close as human beings nigh on impossible. Determined to change that for a time, she dipped down to slip off her shoes. 'We're both due a night free from guilt and the past. A night to run free,' she declared, and with that, she was off.

Picking up her skirts, she ran across coarse European grass that pricked her feet, but it was damp and refreshing, and with each step she took, the sense of freedom increased. An ornate fountain dominated the centre of the lawn. It held the promise of cooling spray, as well as shade and privacy behind its elaborate stonework. The scent of flowers was intoxicating, and so was the thought of the man stalking her. She ran faster and faster into a situation of her own creation, knowing she could be risking everything on an impulse.

She skirted behind the fountain and held her breath. Closing her eyes as she rested back against the cold stone, she knew what she ought to do, when Raffa found her, and that was thank him for a wonderful evening and politely say goodnight, but if she didn't want to take things to the next level, what was she doing here? And if Raffa didn't want the very same thing, why was he coming after her?

Every moment seemed to stretch into an hour, and she almost jumped out of her skin when he finally rounded the fountain. Even in the dark, she felt his black stare on her face. It scorched its way through her body, heating every erotic zone she possessed, but, instead of yanking her into his arms as she'd halfway hoped, Raffa kept his distance, and stared out to sea. Had she misjudged this chemistry between them? Perhaps he didn't feel the same way she did. Maybe she was in danger of making a fool of herself. Upfront as always, she went ahead to find out. 'Kiss me,' she whispered.

'That isn't sensible, Rose.'

'I don't care,' she replied stubbornly.

CHAPTER SIX

THEY DIDN'T KISS right away. Instead, they shared the same breath, the same air, teasing by promising contact, only to pull back. When Raffa finally drove his mouth down on hers, delay and anticipation had built to such a crescendo the outcome was inevitable.

'What, here?' Raffa murmured with surprise as Rose drew him with her to the ground.

'Why not? Or, are you afraid of grass stains?'

He laughed as he joined her, and she sank into an embrace so firm, yet gentle, she had never felt so safe in her life. 'Don't stop?' he confirmed.

There was no stopping, no calming her, either, until she heard a peal of laughter.

'Relax,' Raffa soothed. 'It's only another couple enjoying the fruits of the night. They don't care about us.'

'A fruit of the night?' Rose repeated with a grin. 'Is that what I am?'

Cupping her buttocks in one big hand, Raffa nudged the fine mesh of her gown aside. Exposing her breasts, he suckled each nipple in turn. Thrusting her fingers through his hair, she kept him close. 'Touch me. Touch me here… Show me… Show me what to do.'

'That would be my pleasure,' Raffa whispered as he set about undressing her.

'You really don't care if we're discovered?'

'I really don't,' he admitted in the half growl she loved.

Rose was perfect. Everything about tonight had been perfect. Knowing every inch of Rose intimately was inevitable and right. Planting kisses on her neck, he abraded her skin very gently with his stubble. The thong she was wearing was composed of the finest Swiss lace and yielded easily to his strong fingers. She was so aroused the flimsy fabric could barely contain her. Trailing his fingertips over the site of her arousal, while denying Rose any real pressure, made her fierce. 'Don't tease me,' she warned, attempting to guide his hand to where she wanted it.

'But I enjoy teasing you,' he admitted as he shook her off to continue his lazy exploration.

Thrusting fiercely against his hand, she clung to him, almost in desperation. A complex mix of strong and vulnerable, Rose was unique in his experience. He enjoyed the contrast, but refused to take advantage of it. 'Relax,' he soothed. 'You don't have to rush this or do anything. Leave it all to me.'

She obeyed, moaning in pleasure as he gradually increased the movements of his skilled fingers until she had to stifle her cries of completion.

Having made sure she was completely satisfied, and

knowing he'd always remember the look on her face as she came, he reached for his phone.

'What are you doing?' Rose asked, frowning, still panting with the force of her climax.

'Telling my people to have the helicopter ready to leave right away.'

'You'd leave without saying goodnight to the Prince?' Rose sounded scandalised. 'I should thank him for a wonderful evening,' she insisted. 'I feel bad—'

'There's no need to thank him. The Prince is fully occupied with matters of his own. If it helps you to feel better, you can send him a note tomorrow.'

'I will,' Rose assured him with feeling.

He helped her straighten her clothes. 'We'll pick up your shoes on the way,' he promised, reminding Rose of the high heels she'd discarded.

'I still feel bad, leaving like this,' she admitted with a glance towards the brilliantly lit ballroom.

'The one thing you don't feel is bad,' he said, wrapping a protective arm around her shoulders.

'You could be right,' Rose conceded with a mischievous nod.

Raffa directed the pilot to the second officer's seat, and he flew the helicopter from the palace to the *Pegasus*, while Rose sat in the second row, wondering if it was possible to be any more aware of her body and its needs than she was now. It seemed the more Raffa introduced her to this forbidden pleasure, the more she wanted. She was so greedy for him.

He was tough, rugged and hot-as-hell sexy, and an excellent pilot too. Their landing was barely discernible. One moment they were in the air and the next on the swaying deck of the superyacht. It could have been a metaphor for her life, Rose reflected, now she'd had the chance to quietly and calmly reflect on the events of the night.

'You can take your headphones off now,' Raffa prompted as the second officer bid them goodnight and left.

Not wanting the fairy tale to end, Rose gave herself another blissful moment, before reluctantly doing as Raffa said. She knew that the clock had struck midnight and Cinderella's shoes were now firmly in place. 'What time would you like to meet up tomorrow?' she asked, to demonstrate her understanding that they were back on the boat where things would have to change between them.

'Tomorrow?' Raffa sat back in his seat to shoot her a quizzical look.

'I thought—'

'What did you think, Rose?'

Opening the door, he came around to help her disembark. Moving into his arms felt so right. It was moving out of them that felt wrong, but now they were safe on deck, she imagined they'd be heading off to their own accommodation. How their hands touched, brushed, until finally they linked fingers, she had no idea. It didn't do to examine things too closely sometimes.

'Do you want to call by your room first?'

'No need,' she exclaimed breathlessly.

They almost didn't make it as far as his suite. The moment they were inside the *Pegasus*, Raffa swung her around and thrust her back against the wall. Lodging his fists either side of her face, he kept her in place for a kiss as hungry and as fierce as any she could dream of. The pressure of his body against hers was exciting and arousing, and it was only moments before she was moaning again…noisily.

Raffa was laughing when he released her. 'My security guards will come running.'

'Good! Kiss me again,' she demanded, high on Raffa wanting her.

Their kisses grew increasingly heated until she took Raffa by the hand and dragged him through the ship, laughing, excited and breathless. This was what had been missing in her life, this ability to feel without counting the cost of everything. If she could just have this—him—Raffa—for one, single night, she'd take it, no question.

Shouldering open the door to his suite, Raffa swung Rose into his arms and carried her to the bed. The only thing clear in his head was Rose. She was his focus, and he was determined to make every moment special for her—

But she could still surprise him.

'How d'you do that?' he asked as she gasped out her pleasure. 'All I've done is lie you down on the bed.'

'Maybe it's enough,' she suggested, laughing. 'I really don't know,' she admitted. 'Nothing like this has ever happened to me before, so it's you who must have the knack.'

He drew back. 'Are you saying I'm your first?'

'Not technically,' she admitted, shyly, he thought, for Rose. 'But in every way that matters—' she lifted one shoulder and let it fall again '—you are my first.'

'You'd better explain.' He sounded harsher than he'd intended, but he had no intention of taking Rose if he was her first and there was even the smallest chance that she'd regret it later.

'All right,' she conceded, reading his expression with her usual ease. 'You want the truth? Here it is. You can laugh at me all you like. I'm sure you're going to think me a real country bumpkin, compared to the women you usually date.'

'Stop right there,' he warned. 'I don't think that at all.'

She gave him an assessing look, and then explained. 'Fumbles in the back seat of a car, with someone who knew even less than I did, could never match up to this.'

'That's it?' he pressed, frowning.

'That's it,' she confirmed.

He wanted nothing more than to fold Rose in his arms and kiss her to reassure her, but Rose hadn't finished with her surprises. Reaching for him, she began to deal with the buttons on his shirt, until she lost patience and they went flying everywhere. Tumbling her back on the bed, he kicked off his shoes, unbuckled his belt and snapped it from the loops. This short break gave Rose the chance to leap into a kneeling position in front of him.

'No,' he said firmly. 'This first time is for you.'

'And the next ten thousand are for you?' she teased, breathless with laughter and excitement.

'If you're lucky,' he teased her back. 'But, seriously, Rose,' he murmured after a long, consuming kiss, 'no second thoughts?'

'Are you joking?' she demanded, looking at him with surprise.

'I'm being perfectly serious,' he assured her.

'Resisting you would take more power than I possess.'

'That's what I'm afraid of,' he admitted.

'Let me repay some of the pleasure you've given me,' she implored.

'We'll be here all night.'

'Isn't that the purpose of this?'

Rose's chin was angled as she asked the question, and her eyes were sparkling emerald green. Making her move, she took matters into her own mouth, and he needed every ounce of his self-control to pull back from the intense pleasure that provoked. The answer was to turn her beneath him, before he lost it completely. Removing her dress, he pulled away to admire her naked body, while Rose, indolent and relaxed, rested her arms above her head in an attitude of absolute trust.

'Not so fast,' he warned when she wrapped her legs around him. 'We've got all night.'

* * *

Did they? Rose wondered. This week on Raffa's yacht would soon be over, then they'd sail back to Spain, where the realities of life were waiting. But it was hard to argue when Raffa was moving steadily down her body, dropping kisses along the way.

Slipping a pillow beneath her buttocks, he raised her even higher. Resting her legs on the wide spread of his shoulders, he dipped his head. Every inch of her ached with desire. 'Surely, it's your turn soon?'

'Your pleasure comes first for me.'

'But you're equally important,' she insisted fiercely, before he found a most effective way of silencing her.

'Use me,' Raffa encouraged.

'Like this?' She shivered with extremes of sensation as she tried touching him to the most sensitive part of her body.

'That's not so hard, is it?' Raffa murmured, smiling down.

'It's extremely hard,' she approved, taking him a little way inside her.

'Like this,' he husked against her mouth.

The initial ecstasy of Raffa sinking deeper gave way to frustration when he pulled back. 'What are you doing?'

'Protecting us both,' he explained as he quickly sheathed himself.

He was so gentle and patient, which was good, as he was big and she was small. It didn't seem possible for such a mountain of a man to be so tender, but when he finally sank inside her to the hilt and rotated his hips, she was drawn into a deliciously unavoidable vortex of pleasure.

Much later they threw themselves down on the bed. As they turned to face each other in silence, it was as if they'd both accepted that something more than sex had just occurred.

But the sex had been truly astonishing, Rose silently conceded as she rolled closer to Raffa simply for the pleasure of having him wrap her in his arms. She dozed off for a while, but woke with a start.

'You okay?' Raffa murmured. Drawing her closer, he brushed Rose's tangled hair away from her face.

'I'm fine,' she whispered back, snuggling into his muscular chest as scenes from the past flashed behind her eyes. The thrill the Kelly family experienced whenever her father came up with another of his crazy schemes. But as sure as night followed day, crashing disappointment always followed. The tin on the mantelpiece, where Rose's mother kept her scant savings, would be emptied, and there'd be a call from the pub to say someone was bringing her father home. Was all closeness fated to end that way? Was this bliss she was sharing with Raffa an illusion? Could she trust it? Could she trust anything? What about Raffa? Was all the publicity about the perfect family he'd been a part of before his parents died all a sham too?

And was Rose being selfish, only thinking of herself right now?

'If you're okay, why are you so tense?' he asked, pulling his head back to stare into her eyes.

'Tell me about your parents,' she said.

There was a long pause, and then Raffa began to speak. 'I drove them to the airfield that day. I even helped them with their luggage. I stood and watched as their plane took off. It was our private jet, so there was nothing to stop me going on board to speak to the pilot.'

'Why would you have done that?'

'I don't know—I just…' Raffa shook his head, at a loss for words. 'If I had visited the cockpit, I would have smelled the drink on the pilot and realised something was badly wrong. I could have stopped that flight.' He grew more heated. 'I should have stopped it—told them to get off—'

'But you had no reason to go on board in the first place,' Rose pointed out gently. 'How many of us live with guilt, and what good does it ever do? I could have stepped between my father and mother when they were arguing—snatched the bottle from him, searched out the rest of his seemingly endless supply of booze. He even hid the bottles in the rubbish bin outside, and that was one of the more obvious places. I could have made more effort to find help for both of them, but instead I did as my mother asked, and stayed quiet. I was much more obedient in those days. Only when it was far too late did I learn to speak up.'

'You were young, at school, and then laying the foundations of your career,' Raffa reminded her. 'A career your mother surely wanted you to have.'

'She did,' Rose confirmed. 'But, d'you see what I'm getting at? We can both blame ourselves endlessly, but what good does it do? We've learned from our mistakes, and now it's time to move on.'

'Says you,' he teased as he drew her back into his arms.

The emotion Rose stirred inside him was almost too extreme. Feelings, memories, everything he'd brooded on for years, threatened to escape the carefully built dam. What had really changed was that he suddenly wanted to confront the past head-on, rather than banishing it to some forgotten part of his mind. Rose had done that. Her determination to love and protect those she cared for touched him. He was the instigator, the protector, the hero, and occasionally the villain, the man who had never needed support from anyone, but, in the high-octane setting of a professional polo ranch, someone with heart, as well as an organised mind, was ideal. Rose was that person. He was right to have appointed her Head Groom. Fearless when it came to brushing convention aside, Rose had passion and fire that matched his.

It was only a matter of time before that passion distracted them both once again, and what started out as gentle, soothing caresses turned fiercely demanding. Lavishing attention on her breasts, he teased her nipples into even tighter buds, while Rose writhed against him, seeking the release they both craved. Taking hold of his hand, she brought it down, her intention clear. Rose knew what she wanted, and how to get it too. At his first touch, she claimed her explosive release, and very soon wanted more. 'I'll be quiet this time,' she promised with a teasing grin, forcing him to remember his comment about the security guards.

'Make all the noise you want.' Sex was an exercise at which he excelled, but with Rose it was so much more. He'd never laughed so much, nor found a woman so appealing. They ended up on the floor laughing, and the next minute things turned wild and raw. Every rule went out of the window. Between them, they had rewritten the rules. All he cared about was Rose's pleasure—and all she cared about was his.

It was only later when they were quiet again, he noticed that she was studying him intently. 'Is something wrong, Rose?'

How to tell this man what she was thinking? Rose stared silently into eyes that weren't bloodshot with booze, or narrowed in anger…into a face that was strong, but not cruel.

'Nothing's wrong,' she lied with a gentle smile. Raffa had helped her to understand that sex could be deeply meaningful, as well as fun. To think those fumbles in the back seat of a car had left her with the impression that sex was a waste of time, and why bother? She knew why now. Raffa had shown her what sex could really be like, and how close it could bring two people.

But for how long nagged at the back of her mind.

Pulling his head back, he stared her directly in the

eyes. 'Unhappy thoughts? Hey, come on, or I'll worry about you.'

'Worry? After that?' She laughed to reassure him, but was she as strong as he thought her? Her father's situation was getting worse, and for all he'd done wrong in the past she would never desert him. If she confessed that, Raffa was bound to question Rose's long-term commitment to his team.

'If you need to talk,' he pressed.

'Here? Now?' she teased in an attempt to distract him.

'At any time,' Raffa said, emphatically. 'I'm not so busy that you'll have to come to bed to talk to me.'

'If that's what it takes,' she murmured, resting her cheek against his warm, hard chest.

'I love that you stop at nothing,' Raffa admitted on a smile. 'But if there's something you want to say, I'm listening.'

Like Rose's fear that her father's condition might worsen suddenly? Loyalty to her family prevented her from saying more. 'Nope. I think you've covered it.'

'I'd rather cover you,' Raffa growled as he tumbled Rose on to her back.

Resting on her elbow, Rose watched Raffa sleep. She marvelled at how close they'd become. That was a precious memory to keep safe when their very different worlds split them apart.

A ping on her phone distracted her. Reality had come calling in the form of a text from her brother Declan.

Reading it, she frowned.

Go home now, Rose. You're needed in Ireland.

Rose typed furiously.

Where r u, Dec?

Rome. But Dad needs help right now—before I can get there.

Everything inside Rose tensed. Whatever had happened must be bad.

What's happened?

It's serious, Rose. Only you can drop everything and go right away.

Whether she agreed with that last statement or not, there was no point wishing things were different. She had to leave now. A few more exchanges with her brother proved even more alarming. It turned out that their father was currently cooling his heels in a police cell after rampaging out of control.

Pressing her lips together until they hurt stopped the tears. Everything she had to lose was right here in this room. Tonight was nothing more than stolen time, an indulgence she couldn't afford. Rose's father couldn't look after himself, and both she and Raffa could. That didn't mean that the affection, the laughter, the trust and the care they'd shared meant nothing. She'd never forget it.

Never.

But there was no time for tears—no time for anything but booking a ticket to Ireland.

Don't worry, Dec. I'm on my way.

CHAPTER SEVEN

WITH THE FAIRY TALE well and truly over, Rose slipped out of bed, grateful that Raffa slept on while she debated what to do. Should she wake him and tell him the news? Didn't he have enough on his plate? Leaving a note was better, she decided, but how to explain in a few dry words what last night had meant to her? There weren't enough words—or enough time, she realised with a glance at her watch.

Hunting around, she found pen and paper in the nightstand, and wrote a quick note.

Please forgive me. I didn't want to disturb you. A text from my brother says there's trouble at home. Don't worry, I'll be fine. In touch as soon as possible. R

A member of the crew, accustomed to ferrying strangers of one ilk or another, took her to shore in one of the small, fast boats stored in the hull of the superyacht. From there it would be a cab ride to the airport, and a swift journey home. Fretting as she stared back at the sleek, shadowy form of the *Pegasus*, Rose wished she'd said thank you on the note to Raffa for the opportunities he'd given her…for everything.

She should have known the roller-coaster ride she'd seen her parents take was pretty much the same for everyone. Tightening her hands around the frigid steel rail, she determined to find her way back to the upside of that ride. Wallowing in self-pity was a complete and utter waste of time. What she needed now was resolve and the strength to turn things around.

If you'll have me back once I've found a solution for my father, I'll see you in Spain.

She cast this thought into the wind whipping her hair about, which was about as effective as trying to stem the tears pouring down her face. Action was what was needed now.

A curse of regret, of frustration, of determination, flew out of her mouth. Knuckling her eyes, she stemmed the tears. No way would she stop searching, until she found the answer for her father's addiction, and a way forward for herself.

He woke slowly, basking in sensations of complete satisfaction from the previous night. Reaching for Rose, he found her side of the bed cold. Instantly alert, he sat up to see the sheets had been straightened. The entire suite was silent. Was she back in her stateroom, swotting for that morning's interrogation, as Rose liked to describe his probing into her experience with horses? No one was more dedicated to her work than Rose, and he had yet to find a gap in her knowledge.

Rolling over on the bed, he picked up the phone to call her room. It rang out. His next call was to the purser. It shot him out of bed. Add resourceful to Rose's list of accomplishments, but in this instance, she'd taken things too far, leaving the *Pegasus* by motor launch some time shortly after dawn. His first response was stone-cold anger. How could she leave him without a word after all they'd shared? Was it possible he'd misread her character so badly? He'd told Rose things he'd never told another soul. And she'd trusted him. He had believed the confidences they'd shared had connected them on a deeper level. Obviously, he was wrong.

Had she thrown away the chance to work on his ranch? Was that all it meant to her? *'Gran Dios en el cielo!'* If this was what it meant to have feelings, feelings could go to hell!

He showered and dressed, and only then saw the note. Snatching it up, he read it quickly, then brought it to his face.

What the hell am I doing? Do I think it might contain a trace of her scent?

He gave a bitter laugh at his foolishness.

Trouble at home? What did that mean? Rose had cut him out when he could have helped her. Obviously, she didn't agree. Was this anger the result of a blow to his pride? If Rose was in trouble, she needed him. As a concerned employer he had a duty of care to his employees.

To hell with that! Rose came first, employee or not.

Whatever nightmares the past had held, Rose would never abandon her responsibilities without good reason. She had put her family first, which was exactly what he would have done in her place. Making a call, he filed a flight plan to Ireland.

How would Raffa feel when he read her note? Hurt? Puzzled? Angry?

Rose ground her jaw as the cab took her to the Garda station where her father was being held, knowing it would likely be all of the above. He'd trusted her, and confided in her, and she'd walked out on him, as if the things they'd shared had meant nothing to her. She'd tried texting him, but for some reason the texts wouldn't send. Was Raffa blocking them? Who could blame him? He could only think the worst of her.

She had to put those thoughts aside as the cab slowed and parked up. She'd promised her mother to look after the family, and that was exactly what she'd do.

Spain seemed like a distant dream when Rose learned how bad things were. The officer in charge explained that her father, who was currently sleeping it off in a cell, had assaulted his carers during a drunken rage, and it had taken two strapping members of the Garda to subdue him.

'You can't expect anyone to take care of him outside of a hospital facility,' the officer insisted. 'It's not safe to be around him.'

'I'll take care of him.'

How? How?

The question banged in her brain. This was so much worse than she had imagined. She'd been thinking she'd have to find new carers, now it seemed she might have to take their place, which meant giving up her career—never seeing Raffa again. But, what else could she do, when family was everything?

Lifting her chin, she stared into the officer's eyes. 'He's my father. I love him, and I'm here to take him home.' The how, when and where would have to wait. The deathbed promise Rose had made to her mother would always come first.

She would sort this out, whatever it took, although the bank manager she'd called from the cab had said there was no money in the farm's account. There were no magic wands, either, so she'd begged him for a couple of weeks to sort things out. Thankfully, he'd agreed, but she had two weeks and no longer.

The irony was that Rose had left Ireland in the first place in order to earn enough to keep the farm afloat and pay for her father's care, but now— Her heart lurched with pity and love as her father shambled along the corridor towards her. Everything would have to change, she realised. 'Come on, Dad. Let's take you home.'

Piloting an aircraft calmed Raffa. Learning to fly as a teenager had been a revelation. He'd become a better planner because of it, thorough and more meticulous. Logical decisions became instinctive, when patience was vital, rather than a virtue. The circumstances of his parents' death had brought out the worst in him. Flying had improved his angry resentful clay, fashioning it into something close to a decent human being. Forgiving himself for leaving them that day would never happen, but becoming a pilot had given him the calm he needed to go on. He'd need those qualities in Ireland. His team had supplied more information about her father, which made him even more concerned about Rose.

His jet sliced through the brightening sky on autopilot, giving him the chance to reflect on their time together. Not just the sex, but the quiet times in between, when they'd talked and shared and listened. That was new to him. Zany, beautiful, unique and caring, Rose was a completely new experience for him. She'd willingly sacrifice everything she'd worked so hard for to take charge of her father's care, and she had opened a window on the part of him that had been shuttered for years. Far from regretting the feelings she'd stirred up inside him, he understood why she was racing back to save her father. Family was everything to him too. What that meant for his ranch, and Rose's unparalleled work as his head groom, was something he'd soon discover.

Love was a strange and indelible curse, but overall it was a blessing, Rose concluded, feeling the warm glow of familiarity, with all its upsides and downsides, as the cab splashed through the mud in the yard to pull up outside the familiar ramshackle farmhouse. It had taken all her powers of persuasion to get the driver to take them anywhere with her father still marinated in booze.

Love didn't rely on being fed with regularity, or

even handled with care, Rose concluded as she glanced at her father slumped in the corner of the cab. Love just was, and she loved her father. He wasn't a bad man. He was a weak man. What made it easier to face the future ahead of them was remembering the man who'd cried in her arms when her mother died, the man who knew full well how sick he was. That was the man she'd come home for, the man she'd search heaven and earth for to find him a treatment.

Not that a moment of panic didn't grab her as the taxi driver helped her to manhandle her father out of the cab. But then she remembered Raffa's words. *You don't know how strong you are until you're tested.*

'Come on, Dad. We're home.'

Rose opened the farmhouse door with her father trailing behind. It was hard to know whether to follow his bleary stare and discover where he was hiding the bottles, or go straight on in. Feed him first, she decided, and then go and hunt the bottles.

There could have been no bigger shock when she opened the door. Far from the neglected, cold stone hearth she'd been expecting, a fire was roaring, and the ancient scrubbed table in the centre of the room was loaded with food.

The noise that greeted them was tumultuous. Half the village seemed to have turned up to welcome them home. The warmth of good neighbours embraced her, her father too, and not as the local drunk but as someone in need of compassion and love.

'Ah, you didn't think we'd leave you on your own,'

Máire, the warm-hearted owner of the local bakery, exclaimed as she wafted away Rose's thanks. 'I knew your father when we were at school together, before the drink turned him bad. I'll be taking him to live with me and my boys when you go back to Spain.'

'I can't let you do that,' Rose exclaimed. Her best guess was that Máire's five strapping lads ate the profits of the bakery as it was, and if her father was as violent as the Garda said he was, would any of them be safe?

'But you are going back to Spain?' Máire asked with a worried frown.

'I don't see how I can,' Rose said, shaking her head. 'He's my responsibility—'

'You've got your own life to lead,' Máire said firmly. 'Your father won't get into trouble with me,' she added, wrapping a capable arm around Rose's shoulders. 'My boys will keep him in line. If we can't be neighbourly in a small place like this, what hope is there for the world? And my lads will be only too glad to help you with the horses.'

Great riders, all of them, and kind to their animals, Rose quickly assessed. 'That would be wonderful—' All of Máire's suggestions would be wonderful, but Rose had never turned her back on a problem yet. 'Maybe in the short term,' she reluctantly agreed. 'And I can't tell you how grateful I am, but I'll be paying for your time—'

'That won't be necessary.'

Everyone turned to face the door.

'Raffa?'

Stunned rigid, Rose's brain simply refused to compute the fact that Raffa Acosta was framed in the doorway of the ramshackle farmhouse where she'd grown up.

Her face heated up in response to his level black stare. The last time she'd seen him, he was sprawled naked across the bed they'd shared. 'You're here,' she managed lamely.

'Evidently,' he agreed blandly.

Private jet. Fast car waiting on the tarmac, Rose's brain rapidly deduced. The sight of him, hair rumpled as if he'd got out of bed and come straight here, not even bothering to tuck in his top properly, sent a bolt of lust straight to her core. Jeans, boots and a leather jacket with the collar both up and down completed the picture of a man whose world could shift at the speed of light.

'Let me get you a drink,' Máire offered, stepping in between them to break the awkward moment. No one else spoke. They were too busy staring at superstar Raffa Acosta, a man of myth and legend in a village where horses, and everything connected to them, were practically a second religion.

'Would coffee be possible?' Raffa suggested, his gaze not wavering from Rose's face for a moment.

'Why don't I get you a glass of water while you wait for the coffee to brew?' Rose suggested, glad of any excuse to escape that burning stare.

'Did you know he was coming?' she whispered discreetly to Máire.

'Declan said—'

'Declan?' Rose interrupted with surprise. 'Raffa's been speaking to my brothers?'

'There's no law against it, as far as I know,' Máire told her with a shrug. 'Apparently, your man has business in Ireland.'

'He's not my man,' Rose whispered hotly, and just as fast she regretted the outburst. 'Sorry, Máire—I just didn't expect to see him here.'

Was she that business, or did Raffa have other plans? Rose wondered, conscious of his stare on her back. When she handed him the water, he was careful not to touch her, she noticed. She couldn't blame him. Lifting her chin, she confronted the harshness in his eyes. 'Well, this is a surprise,' she murmured.

'Isn't it?' he bit out.

'You read my note?'

'I wouldn't be here otherwise.'

'I'm sorry for the way I left.'

'Why didn't you wake me?'

Rose opened her arms in a helpless gesture. 'What could you have done?'

'I could have brought you here, for a start,' Raffa ground out as he backed her into a shadowy corner, out of earshot of the rest.

'I can—'

'Manage very well on your own?' he suggested with impatience. 'Can you care for your father, when he's in one of his drunken rages?'

Raffa knew everything, Rose realised. His team must have filled him in. How it must have hurt him to be reminded of the dangers of drink. The fury she could see in his eyes was that of a much younger man. He was remembering a tragedy from years back. The incident with her father had only increased his pain tenfold.

'Will you stay home twenty-four-seven to make sure he doesn't hurt himself—or you?' he raged. 'Are you prepared to sacrifice everything you've worked so hard for? How do you intend to magic up the money for his care? And he will need care. Your father needs professional help, Rose. You can't help him, or you'd have done it long before now.'

'I can love him,' she countered fiercely. 'And Máire's offered to help—they were at school together. She's one of the few people he trusts, and her sons can handle him until I find him the type of care he needs.' Touching Raffa's arm to reach him, to offer him consolation, only resulted in him shaking her off.

'That's a very kind offer from a neighbour, but you know it's only a short-term solution. What about your job with me, Rose?'

'Can we talk outside?' She understood why Raffa sounded so harsh, and why there was no warmth in his eyes, so it was a relief when he agreed.

She led the way, and didn't stop walking until they'd left the farmyard behind, and were at least half a mile down the road. There was a tree that looked a bit like an umbrella. It acted as a sunshade in the summer. Today it was a leaky umbrella, and Rose hadn't thought to bring a coat.

'Here. Take this,' Raffa growled when she hugged

herself and shivered. Shrugging off his jacket, he draped it around her shoulders. It still held his warmth.

'I will need time off,' she admitted, dragging the jacket closer, 'but I promise to make it up to you.'

There was no reaction from Raffa. This was worse than talking to the boss. It was like talking to a stranger. It was impossible to believe she'd been wrapped in his arms only a few hours before, when he was as remote and aloof as this.

The past had done that. It had damaged them both, and now she was hanging on to her career by a rapidly fraying thread.

'What if I take my holiday leave to try and sort this out?' she offered. 'Would you allow me to do that?'

'And you'll restart, when?' Raffa asked, still without a shred of warmth in his voice. 'At *your* convenience?'

'No,' Rose protested. 'I'll stick strictly to schedule.'

'And how will you make that happen? You can give me no guarantees,' he exclaimed angrily. 'A few lines on a scrap of paper to explain your sudden departure? Why should I trust you?'

'I promise I'll return as soon as I can.'

His look chilled her. 'You say that now,' he rasped.

The distance between them had never seemed greater. The closeness they'd shared seemed to have completely disappeared, but she couldn't let it go without a fight. 'How long are you staying in Ireland?'

Raffa's brow furrowed. 'Why do you want to know?'

She had no right to know, but having him close to

her was like having a rock to moor her ship to. A ship that had been well and truly holed beneath the water-line. She'd picked herself up many times before, but not like this, not with her heart in tiny pieces.

'You should go back to the house,' Raffa insisted in the same emotion-free tone. 'Your neighbours have gone to a lot of trouble to welcome you home.'

'You're not leaving already?' Rose's voice hitched on the words.

'No, but the party isn't for me, and I'll only distract you from the welcome your friends want to give you, and that wouldn't be right.'

'We'll speak again, though?' She'd be begging next.

'We will,' he confirmed.

Where and when was never mentioned, leaving nothing but doubt in Rose's mind. Career or family? Those were her choices, and family won through every time. There'd been a glimmer, just a glimmer of possi-bility that she could finally live her own life, love, and thrive, and... Do what? *Live selfishly?* Was that what she wanted? No. Of course it wasn't. She'd sacrificed all thought of romantic relationships in the past, and that was what she'd do again now.

Is it the right thing to do, or is it cowardice? Am I frightened of risking my heart? My parents' rela-tionship turned into a living hell. Am I incapable of believing I can do things differently? Where's my courage gone? Where's the determination that brought me to Spain, to support that very family and further my career? Is that all spent now?

'You'll find me at the inn,' Raffa said, shaking Rose back to reality. 'If you need me, call.'

I need you now, thought the woman who'd always managed everything on her own. 'I have your number,' Rose confirmed.

'And meet me tomorrow. Nine o'clock at the inn.'

Raffa raised a hand as he walked away. He didn't turn around.

CHAPTER EIGHT

'*Dios!*' HE WAS pacing his room at the inn like a caged animal. From having no feelings to *this*?

The moment he'd seen Rose with her father, any anger he'd felt at her desertion had swung to concern for a valued member of staff. A drunken father—a drunken pilot—the connection was unavoidable. This was his worst nightmare come true.

But he wasn't standing by helpless this time. He'd summed up the situation at the farmhouse in a glance. The old man needed more help than either Rose or her neighbours could give him, which was all the more reason for Raffa to bring forward his plans. He glanced at his watch. Rose was due shortly. The inn was close to her farm. Sleep had eluded him, but that was no fault of the warm-hearted landlady. The accommodation was more than adequate. Bed. Bathroom. Desk. What more did he need?

He'd reserved a private room downstairs for his meeting with Rose. This was no romantic tryst, but the venue for a serious talk. She couldn't just take off whenever she felt like it. There was a process to be followed, as Rose well knew. He relied on his staff, particularly someone entrusted with one of the most vital jobs. The only reason he was prepared to cut Rose some slack was because no one understood loyalty to family better than he. Hearing a door open and close, and the murmur of voices, he headed downstairs. Rose brought the chill of morning with her, along with her familiar wildflower scent. She looked tense. He barely had a chance to say hello before the landlady he'd struck a deal with to buy the inn bustled forward.

'I've prepared the room as you asked.' She beamed. 'Your room now, Señor Acosta. If there's anything else I can get you?'

'Nothing,' he said briskly. 'Thank you. I'm sure everything will be fine.'

He'd planned to tell Rose about his purchase of the inn at a more appropriate time. Now she looked shocked. It couldn't be helped. In his world things moved quickly. In this instance that speed could only benefit Rose. 'Come in,' he invited, noting how pale she looked.

'This is *your* room?' Rose challenged the moment the door was shut.

He allowed himself a moment of pleasure at the fact that a fire had been lit and two battered leather armchairs, made more inviting with the addition of hand-sewn cushions, had been drawn up either side. These were good people, full of good intentions. 'I'll answer your questions later,' he promised, indicating one of the seats. 'Have you had breakfast?'

'I don't want to eat,' Rose told him in a clipped

tone. 'I'd rather get this over with. If you're going to fire me, please don't draw it out.'

'I've brought you here to discuss your future on my ranch.'

More colour drained from her cheeks.

'Rose, listen to me before you draw any conclusions. I'm going to call for coffee, toast and eggs. You're no good to me in pieces. I know the situation at home is hard, but you don't have to battle through this on your own.'

'And then you'll fire me,' she said confidently.

'There's a process to follow on my yard, as you well know. I'm not firing you. Gross misconduct would call for instant dismissal, and I hardly think leaving my bed in the early hours fits the bill.' Rose's jaw worked, but she said nothing. 'You'll get through this,' he promised, 'but you can't disappear on a whim. If something important happens outside work, all the more reason to come to me and explain why you're worried. That's what I'm here for.'

Her green eyes turned dark with emotion. 'So, you're not sacking me.'

'I just said so. This is simply a reminder that the position of Head Groom can't be left empty for long.'

'I don't expect it to be. Adena will cover for me. And, please believe me, I didn't anticipate any of this.'

'But you must have known how sick your father was, and yet you didn't tell me.'

'How could I tell you under these particular circumstances, knowing I'd only add to your grief over your own parents?'

'I think I can handle it.'

'Can you?'

She looked so concerned, he couldn't be angry with her. Everything she did, all she had ever done, was always for the good of other people. On that thought he called for breakfast. She looked as if she hadn't eaten properly in days.

'It's been a race against time,' she confessed. 'Save enough money for my father's care, or stay here to care for him without any money. Those were my choices. I foolishly thought I'd have sufficient funds in time to save him.'

'You can't live your life playing catch-up, Rose.'

'Tell me about it,' she agreed with a humourless laugh. Straightening up, she raised her chin bravely. 'So, the pub belongs to you now?'

'It does,' he confirmed.

'There's just so much to take in. I couldn't believe it when you arrived last night. What are you up to, Raffa?'

'I'm here on business.'

'Buying up the village, and fitting in some pastoral care at the same time? I'm sorry,' Rose added quickly, with a gesture suggesting she'd do anything to undo those words. 'I've no right to question you. It's just that our situation is so complicated.'

'No, it isn't. If I can keep my personal and professional lives apart, so can you. I'm offering you a way forward. Take your holiday entitlement if you need to, but don't shut me out. As your employer, I'll support you any way I can, but the position of Head Groom must be filled—if not by you, then by someone else.'

Dios! What was he saying? This wasn't about business, it was all about Rose. He wanted to help her as much as he could, but she wouldn't let him.

'I appreciate you giving me a second chance,' she said, matching his formal tone. 'I'd like to take you up on the offer.'

With that, she got up and left the room, leaving him to smash his fist into the table with frustration.

'I hope I'm not too late,' the landlady announced within moments of Rose leaving as she backed into the room with a loaded tray of food.

'Just leave it on the table, thank you.'

He could think of nothing but Rose—chin up, shoulders back, typical Rose, ready to take on the next challenge and the next. Her fighting spirit would see her through, but she couldn't go on like this forever. If she refused his help, he'd watch from the wings, ready to catch her if she fell. He would always care for Rose, even from a distance.

Care was a strange word, very close to love…

And didn't he destroy those he loved?

Not this time. He couldn't fix everything, but nothing on earth would stop him caring for Rose.

Rose went straight from the meeting with Raffa to check on her father, who was living with Máire and her boys at the bakery. Rose was looking forward to seeing him, and dreading it too. She never knew what to expect, and it was impossible to be in his company without feeling such regret for the man he might have been. Máire had said he was responding well to the discipline her sons imposed, but, as Raffa had pointed out, that only was a temporary solution. Relationships were rarely straightforward, she reflected as she walked down the village street. With the threat of dismissal removed, Rose was relieved, but not comforted. Nothing could compensate for losing the closeness she'd so briefly experienced with Raffa, and his new formality had left her feeling she'd lost something precious that she might never get back. *You can't have everything*, she told herself firmly as she knocked on Máire's door. That would be greedy.

'I've given your father the small bedroom directly above the bakery,' Máire explained as she welcomed Rose inside. 'It has its own bathroom, and there's no access to either exit without going past my room,' she added with a wink. 'But he's out with my boys at the moment. You'll stay for a mug of tea?'

'Will they be long?' Rose asked with concern, picturing the wreck of a man she'd brought home from the police cell. News that her father was out with Máire's strapping lads might either herald a turning point or a chance for him to escape the bakery to sneak off for a drink. Whichever it was, Rose had good cause to worry.

'They'll walk him to death, if they don't work him to death first,' Máire confided. 'And they're on top of his drinking. They got their own father sober, remember?'

Rose hummed diplomatically. She remembered

Máire's husband stopping the drink, but she also remembered him running off with the vicar's wife afterwards.

'Your father had too much time on his hands to think about your mother, and he'll not get a drink here,' Máire reassured her. 'So, you go find that meal of a man, and ask about his plans for the hall—'

'The *hall*?' Rose tensed. 'Don't you mean the pub?'

Máire laughed as if Rose had just said the funniest thing. 'Pub, the hall—who knows what else he's bought up in the village? By the time Señor Acosta's finished here, we'll all be dancing the flamenco and snapping our castanets.'

His team was well on with the purchase of the Old Hall. He hadn't mentioned it to Rose, as he didn't want to raise her hopes until the deal was done. The large baronial-style building was perfect for one of his sister's retreats. He couldn't wait to tell Sofia what he'd found.

'You do know I'm still on my honeymoon?' Sofia complained with her usual good humour.

Hearing a steel band in the background, he drew his own conclusions. Her husband, Cesar, had never stinted on exotic hideaways. He'd probably bought a new island for his bride. 'This won't take long.'

'Just don't buy up everything in the village,' Sofia said with concern when he explained his plan, 'or Rose might think you're taking over. Don't hurt her, Raffa. She's got more than enough to put up with.'

Sofia and Rose had enjoyed some quiet time in the

run-up to the wedding, with plenty of chance to unload. 'I've no intention of hurting anyone. I'm helping by—'

'Buying up everything?' his sister suggested dryly. 'May I humbly suggest that might not work where Rose is concerned?'

'The Old Hall will make an excellent retreat.'

'My first in Ireland,' his sister reflected thoughtfully. 'Why not?'

Sofia was forced to agree. 'For once, I can't think of a single reason to argue with you.'

'Which must mean it's time for you to get back to enjoying your honeymoon, while I put these ideas into action.'

'Explain your plan carefully to Rose. She won't thank you for throwing your money around, unless she understands why you're doing it. Rose is determined to stand on her own two feet, and I admire her for it.'

'You like her?'

'I like her a lot,' Sofia confirmed, 'and I want you to be happy, but that means taking off your blinkers to see things from Rose's point of view. Can you do that, Raffa?'

He refused to be drawn on the subject of Rose.

'You want me to butt out of your love life?' Sofia suggested.

'I don't need your advice,' he confirmed.

'True,' she said. 'You need crowd control.'

Ice rushed through Rose's veins as she clutched her phone to her face. Her oldest brother, Declan, was on the other end of the line, telling Rose that Raffa Acosta had indeed bought the Old Hall. What next? she wondered, though in fairness the building had been derelict for some time, with no sign of anyone with either the money or the inclination to restore what had once been a thriving estate. 'How do you know this?'

'He phoned me. The man himself,' Declan explained, sounding as pleased as Punch.

'Raffa Acosta phoned you?' Rose's brow pleated in puzzlement. Raffa hadn't said a word to her. 'What else did he say?' she asked suspiciously.

'He'll be making an offer for the farm next,' Declan said, in what Declan would call his 'only half joking' voice.

There was no joke about it, as far as Rose was concerned. 'And you think that's a good idea?'

'It would be a solution,' Declan confessed. 'It would let you off the hook, for a start.'

'I don't want to be let off the hook.'

'Why do you keep on supporting our father, after the way he treated you and our mother?'

And my brothers, Rose thought, taking a moment to revisit the past before returning her attention to the call. 'He's ill, Dec. Alcoholism is an illness. Our father needs help, not blame. If we did sell the farm, I'm frightened the shock might tip him over the edge. I can't just let that happen, and then walk out on him.'

'That's easy to say when he's not trying to knock your teeth out.'

'He'd never do that to me,' Rose declared. 'All that bluff and bluster was just the drink talking.'

'He'd only have to fall on you, to knock you out flat.'

'I think I'm a bit nimbler on my feet than he is. Look, I'll get back to you, Dec,' Rose soothed, knowing Declan was remembering things in the past that couldn't help either of them now. 'I'll let you know what I find out,' she promised.

Raffa was buying up the Old Hall as well as the pub? Rose's heart pounded like a jackhammer at the thought. What was he up to? He'd admitted he was in Ireland for business. That had stung at the time, but now the possibility of selling the farm had entered her mind, she was forced to consider it. The money it raised would allow her father to have the best treatment, while her brothers would each get a stake to plough into a business of their own. With Raffa at the helm, the farm animals would have the best care, and the land would be maintained to the highest standard. Was it such a bad idea? There was no point dwelling on it now. She had to speak to Raffa.

'A new era unfolds!' the landlady at the pub exclaimed the moment she heard Rose's voice. 'Señor Acosta is not only keeping us all on, he's increasing our wages. What a marvel he is, Rose. The man hasn't stopped all day.'

No, Raffa had definitely been busy, Rose reflected tensely as she replayed the conversation with Declan. 'If he's still there, I'm coming over to speak to him. See you soon—' Before the landlady had a chance to answer, Rose had cut the line, grabbed her battered waxed jacket from the hook behind the door, and was on her way to confront a man causing more uproar in the village than if aliens had landed.

There was no doubt Raffa could do a lot for the area. Equally, trying to stop him doing anything people in the village disagreed with would be like trying to stop a juggernaut in its tracks.

Ideas flooded Rose's mind. Digging out her phone with frozen fingers, she placed a call, and hurried on. She'd barely walked half a mile when she heard a powerful engine approaching. Pressing back into the bare twigs of the hedge, she gasped with shock as the vehicle roared past, shooting filthy water into her face. There was only one man who could afford to drive a car like that around here. Boss or not, she shook her fist at the disappearing tail lights. The SUV screeched to a halt. Raffa must have seen her through the rearview mirror. Good job he hadn't heard her swearing at him. Mud-drenched, she stalked towards him. Not only was Raffa Acosta a control freak, who thought he could buy up Rose's home town, he was also, she reluctantly noted as he opened the driver's window, the hottest guy this side of hell.

'What do you think you're doing?' she blazed on a breath tense with anger.

'I wanted to see you.'

'Well, now you've seen me, what d'you think?' She held out her arms, to reveal the extent of her soaking.

'You need a bath?' Raffa suggested in a husky drawl that would have made her toes curl, if they hadn't been frozen solid in her boots.

'Hop in, Rose. You'll be warm in here.'

'You'll be seared to a crisp if I climb in beside you. Where do you think you are? A racetrack?'

'Truce?' Raffa suggested, with a look in his eyes and a curve to his sinfully sensuous mouth that brought a rush of inconvenient memories of the hot kind flooding back. 'Truce as far as the farmhouse, at least,' he amended. 'I'm here to repent.'

Rose hummed.

'When you're clean and warm again, I'll explain. Meanwhile…' leaning across the cab, he opened the passenger door '…jump in.'

She was freezing cold, covered in mud and still furious, but the draught of warm air from the interior of the cab was fragrant with the spicy aroma of Raffa. 'There'll be a surcharge for valeting the vehicle,' she warned.

A smile flickered at one corner of his mouth. 'I think I can cover it. Get in, Rose…'

Sometimes it was better to admit you needed help and just say thank you. And if ever there'd been a time to be swept into the rock-solid warmth of Raffa's world, however temporary a stay that might be, this was it.

CHAPTER NINE

HE DROVE SLOWLY to the farmhouse with the heater turned up high. It felt good to cross swords with Rose again, good to have her close. He hadn't forgotten anything, not the way she felt in his arms, or how generous she was in bed, in life, in everything. Or how she'd annoyed the hell out of him by leaving the *Pegasus* so abruptly.

Things were moving faster than expected on the acquisition front, and, from the tense way she was holding herself, he guessed Rose had already spoken to her brother. It wasn't just the shock of a soaking making that chin jut out or those emerald eyes blaze like jewels. He had wanted to be the one to tell Rose of his plans for the village, but only when everything was settled. Raising her hopes would be cruel. He'd hoped his plans for Declan would reassure her. No one knew the land, or how to care for it, better than Declan Kelly. He'd moved fast to secure her brother's services.

He glanced across at Rose, sitting bolt upright in her seat. He'd do anything to persuade her not to sacrifice her life for a duty that no longer existed. Rose's father was going to receive the best possible care, and her brothers could take care of themselves.

Drawing to a halt outside the front door of the farmhouse, he jumped down to help her out. She didn't wait for that, and pushed past him to the front door. He lingered behind for a moment to give her a chance to compose herself before following her inside.

'Do you mind?' he asked, peeling off his jacket. He glanced at the drying rack in front of the hearth.

'Be my guest,' she told him in a clipped tone.

'Shall we sit down?' he suggested.

'Of course,' she agreed. 'Tea?'

'Coffee, if you still have some.'

'Tea it is, then.'

Lifting her chin as she went about her business, Rose reminded him why he was determined to keep this strong, dependable, amusing, quirky and impossible woman in his life.

'What are you doing here, Raffa?' she asked him bluntly as she placed a mug of tea in front of him, so strong he was sure the spoon could stand up in it. 'What are you really doing here?'

'I'm here on business. If you want to take a shower,' he added with a relaxed gesture towards the staircase, 'go right ahead. You must be uncomfortable soaked in mud, and I'm happy to wait.' The tip of her nose was red, and her cheeks were whipped scarlet by the wind. She had never looked lovelier to him.

Ignoring his suggestion, she launched straight in. 'Buying the pub, and then the Old Hall. Is the farm next?'

I thought I could trust you, but now I know I can't.

That was what blazed from her angry expression.

'I haven't done anything underhand, Rose. The Old Hall was for sale, and it's perfect for our needs.'

'*Our* needs?' she queried suspiciously.

'I didn't want to raise your hopes until everything was in place.'

'Raise my hopes about what?' she demanded, frowning.

'I believe, as does Sofia, that the Old Hall would be perfect for one of my sister's retreats.'

Rose looked shocked. 'A retreat in Ireland?'

'Why not? Extra accommodation at the inn for patients attending for assessment, or for staff coming here for interview. I'd say the set-up is perfect,' he confirmed.

Rose's expression was utterly transformed. 'Are you serious?' she asked, as if hardly daring to hope.

'Yes.' He sounded calm, but inwardly he was in turmoil. Nothing mattered more to him than Rose. The thought of not seeing her again was unacceptable to him. Somewhere along the way, between the humour they'd shared and the verbal battles they'd indulged in, as well as their night of passion, a change had happened, but she wasn't ready to hear that yet, any more than he was ready to say the words she wanted to hear. 'I need a head groom,' he said instead. 'You need a solution for your father.'

'You'd build a retreat in Ireland to get me back to Spain?'

'Yes,' he admitted with a one-shouldered shrug.

'So, I'm another of your charities.' She bristled. 'I don't mean to be ungrateful, Raffa, but I know how you love a good cause.'

'Your father won't be the only one to benefit from it, Rose.'

'I'm sorry.' Mashing her lips together, she turned her head to avoid his gaze. 'I shouldn't get so het up. It's just that I don't know what to say.'

'Don't say anything—except, "I'm coming back to Spain."'

'Is this leading to an offer for the farm?' she asked suspiciously.

'Declan does have an interest in selling the farm,' he admitted.

'So, it's all been decided without any input from me?'

'No. Of course it hasn't. You and your brothers would all have to agree to sell.'

'How many have you talked into the deal so far?'

'There's just you to persuade now,' he admitted.

'So, I'm the last to hear.'

'You've been through so much—'

'Don't—don't do that!' She held up her hand as if warding him off. 'Don't say you're protecting me. I'm not the baby sister. Treat me as I deserve to be treated, with the same respect you show my brothers.'

'That has always been my intention, which is why I'm here to talk about it in person.'

'If you approach it the right way, selling the farm could be an answer to our problems,' she conceded. 'It's not what I want, but I have to be pragmatic. My father needs money spending on his care, and the farm could provide that.' Lifting her chin, she stared him in the eyes. Beneath the bravado, he saw a young woman struggling to hold everything and everyone together. Crushed beneath the weight of perceived duty, Rose had yet to come to terms with the fact that she was no longer needed by her brothers as she had been in the past.

'Whatever happens in the future, the Kelly name will remain above the farm,' he pledged.

'With the Acosta brand on every horse, man and drystone wall?' Rose suggested as the enormity of the sale of her family's farm overwhelmed her.

'Don't think of me as a wrecking ball. These purchases are the fastest way to help you and your brothers, as well as your father, and others like him. All I ask is that you see the broader picture and take your feelings for me out of it.'

But she couldn't. Some sort of dam had burst inside her, and a wall of pure emotion hit him square in the chest as Rose sprang up and shoved her chair back so hard it crashed to the floor. He'd never seen her like this before, hands shaking, face drawn. Trapped between a past she couldn't change and a future she couldn't see her way clear to reaching, Rose was as close to a breaking point as anyone could be. He stood in the same instant, ready to catch, soothe or deflect blows, if that was what it came to.

'You don't have to do everything on your own, Rose. Accept help when it's offered. You have no difficulty accepting help for your father. Why can't you accept help from me?'

'Because my father's situation at the bakery is temporary until he starts treatment, while your suggestion means permanent change.'

'Is that such a bad thing?'

'It narrows down my options, and my brothers' options too.'

'What if I told you that I've asked Declan to manage the farm?'

Rose's lips turned white. 'So, it is all decided. I was going to ask you who would pay for Declan to come home, but there's no need for that, is there? Because you've already arranged it. You're like the hub of a wheel, directing us all around you—how fast we move, where we go, and when.'

'No. That's not what I'm doing. Forgive me, Rose, but I thought you wanted to work on my ranch. Clearly, I was wrong.'

'I did—I do.'

Rose clutched her head as if that were the way to shake an answer into it. He longed to take her in his arms, to offer her comfort, but he knew that would only make things worse. 'Go take your shower,' he said instead. 'Don't rush. I'll still be here when you come down.'

It took Rose a good minute to regain her composure, then, firming her jaw, she nodded in agreement. She was on her way across the room to the staircase, leading to what he guessed would be spotlessly clean but basic facilities, when she caught her foot on the edge of a rug. Launching himself across the kitchen, he snatched her into his arms before she hit the ground. Steadying her on her feet, he gave her a chance to recover from the shock.

'Thank you.'

Her voice was shaking, and he flinched inwardly to see Rose so utterly at a loss. 'There's no need to thank me. I'm here for you.'

'Are you?'

She searched his eyes in a way that took hold of his stone-cold heart and fired it into life. Feelings they had both fought so hard to subdue suddenly overwhelmed them, and they crashed together with longing and urgency. But this was Rose. He shouldn't have been surprised when she pulled back.

Raking her hair away from her flushed face, she said calmly, 'Welcome to Ireland, Raffa. I hope you find everything you're looking for here.'

'I have,' he gritted out.

Cupping her face, he drove his mouth down on hers. When he pulled back, the look that blazed between them had nothing to do with employer and employee— or whether or not he was interested in buying property in Ireland. It was primal and deep, and easily eclipsed his desire to plant a stake in Rose's beautiful homeland. 'You taste of mud,' he commented wryly when they paused for breath.

'And you taste of everything I should avoid,' Rose fired back.

'You don't want to avoid me, or why are you here?'

'Because this is my home?'

But Raffa was right. This might be the most misguided thing she'd ever done, but who was going to stop them? Life was measured in moments, some good, some bad, and Rose had learned to grab the good ones and hold on tight. Practical problems could wait. She didn't want tender or teasing. She wanted hot, hard and now, the type of sex that blotted out everything in an explosion of furious passion.

Bodies collided as they cleaved to each other again. Hooking one leg around hers, Raffa thrust her back on top of the kitchen table. Moving between her legs, he undressed her with his usual efficiency. Unfastening his zipper, he used one arm to pillow her head, while his black eyes blazed a promise into hers. That promise of forgetfulness and oblivion was enough for Rose to cry out and claim it right away. Swept into a vortex of pleasure, she rejoiced to be lost. This was appetite pure and simple.

Consumed by arousal, the decision had moved out of their hands. Rose's senses took the lead, while Raffa's experience proved the route map. Even when she begged him for release, he knew how big he was and how carefully he must proceed. That wouldn't do for Rose, not when her heart, soul and body were so utterly his. Grabbing his biceps, she groaned her approval in response to the silky pass of something warm and smooth between her legs. Closing her eyes to concentrate on sensation, she exhaled on a shaking breath when he made a second pass, allowing the tip to catch inside her.

'Again?' he suggested.

'And again,' she agreed, plunging into an abyss of pleasure that left her gasping for breath as he finally took her to the hilt.

One powerful release could never be enough—not

when every inch of Rose was tuned to Raffa's frequency. *'Yes!'* she breathed out again, moving fiercely with him.

Sweeping everything off the kitchen table, he lifted her legs and wrapped them around his waist so he could move more freely, and with even greater force. The vibrations rocked the table halfway across the room, while Rose exclaimed rhythmically with pleasure each time he dealt her a firm, effective stroke. Even the sounds they made were arousing, as was the sight of Raffa staring down at her, clearly enjoying himself. 'Don't stop!' she warned. 'Don't—' He didn't give her a chance to finish before upping the tempo, which drove her straight over the edge.

'Are you okay?' he asked as she dragged in some noisy breaths. Cupping her chin, he stared into her eyes. 'Rose… I didn't hurt you, did I?'

'Hurt me?' His question touched her. Reaching up, she rasped the palm of her hand against his stubble-roughened cheek. 'Of course you didn't hurt me. That was…amazing.'

'Watch the flattery,' he warned with a smile.

She loved the look between them that said they understood each other again. The problems hadn't gone away, but nothing could get in the way of these precious moments.

'Your face is smeared with mud,' she observed, smiling into his eyes.

'I'll take that as a compliment, as yours is too. Is it time for that shower now?'

'Could be,' Rose agreed, grinning as Raffa swung

her into his arms. 'It won't be the type of facility you're used to,' she warned as he jogged up the stairs.

'Running water's all we need.'

Apart from each other, she thought.

Shouldering the door to the bathroom, he turned on the shower. Only now did Rose remember she'd forgotten to flip the switch to heat up the water. 'We're going to freeze,' she warned as Raffa stripped off his clothes.

'Not a chance.' Lifting her into the small cubicle, he secured her arms above her head, nudged his way between her thighs and proved he was right.

If everything could be solved by sex, they'd have the answers to all the world's problems, Rose reflected the next morning. If she had the answer to the doubts etched on her heart by the past, she'd make nothing of the fact that Raffa had already left, leaving his side of the bed cold. Picking up the note he'd left on the pillow, she hardly dared read it. Man up! He was hardly the type to sneak off in the night.

As she had?

Rose growled with impatience, hoping that wouldn't be something else to plague her for the rest of her life. She'd had her reasons. Raffa must have his.

She read the scrawled note.

Not tit for tat. Time to get back to business. R

What had she expected? A declaration of love?

Her body was still throbbing from the attentions of an extraordinary lover, but fabulous sex did not a relationship make. A future between billionaire polo player Raffa Acosta and Rose Kelly, penniless groom? How likely did that seem? Fairy tales didn't happen in real life. And it was a bit too late to worry about getting in too deep where Raffa was concerned. She was already in over her head, with her heart and soul fully engaged. If there was some way to stop that, it remained a mystery to Rose.

Showered and dressed, she made her way down to the kitchen. Expecting the room to be cold, and the fire to be out, she was surprised to find logs blazing in the hearth, and a fresh pot of coffee on the table. And another note.

This is to help you break that tea habit. I can't stand the stuff. R

Smiling and crying at the same time, she brought the note to her chest. She already missed his sense of humour and Raffa's caring ways most of all, but she didn't have a clue where he was, what he was up to or how long he'd be away.

Closing her fist around the note as a torrent of longing and uncertainty overwhelmed her, Rose knew, whatever Raffa was planning, her father had to take priority over her feelings.

Crossing to her mother's desk, she selected a piece of writing paper and began to write. Then stopped. It took time to deliver a letter. Raffa could be halfway across the world. She'd send a text instead. Even that took an age. Could they ever resolve the gulf between them? Rose doubted it. She refused charity, while Raffa liked to handle the reins, not share them. She could only be sure of one thing as she placed a call to Sofia. Telling her heart to forget Raffa Acosta was a waste of time, when her heart remained set on having him.

CHAPTER TEN

THE SKY WAS dark when he left the farm. Being with Rose last night had only spurred on his plan. The past controlled Rose, as it had controlled him, and he was determined they would both move forward. Fate had always seemed his enemy before, but fate had brought him Rose. As Head Groom, she could travel with him, be with him, sleep with him too.

That might make a sad sort of sense, but he couldn't see Rose in the role of convenient mistress. He'd seen her with the children on the ranch—playing with them, teaching them, spending time with them out of choice. Rose wanted more than to be any man's plaything. And she deserved more too. Saving her father while shoehorning in a career was an impossible ask. Plus, she'd be a lousy mistress, he concluded with amusement as he jumped into the SUV. Weren't mistresses supposed to be compliant? Good luck with that! Rose would have her say whatever the situation. His smile broadened at the thought.

Rain lashed the windscreen, throwing up plumes of mud behind the vehicle. The rotten weather matched his mood. Nothing was the same without Rose. She entertained him, touched him, moved him, as no one had. He had to find a way to make this work without promising more than he could offer. It would be far easier to walk away and keep his emotions safe under lock and key, as he always had, but Rose had already made that impossible.

A chord from his phone distracted him as he pulled up in front of the pub. Switching off the engine, he scanned the text.

Rose was offering her resignation? Not on his watch. He texted back.

I don't accept this. I offered you two weeks' holiday leave to sort things out. Use them. R

Every detail of how Rose had tasted when he'd kissed her, and how eagerly she had pressed her body against his, crashed into his mind. Thundering his fist down on the wheel, he gave way to the force of his frustration in a roar. So much for keeping his emotions under lock and key! One thing was certain: Rose stayed in his life. She was too important for anything else. Okay, so the details were sketchy, but details could wait. He'd think about the pros and cons later. Kicking the engine into life, he wheeled the vehicle around to drive back to the farm.

After a successful call to Sofia, Rose hugged her phone close, knowing she should be thrilled at the chance for her father to recover drawing closer. And she would be thrilled, if overshadowing that hadn't been the knowledge that Rose couldn't have everything. Implementing her plan for animal therapy programmes, a plan she hoped would help her father find a renewed sense of purpose, would take longer than two weeks of holiday entitlement, which left her with no alternative but to resign from her post on Raffa's ranch. The thought of breaking from him, disappointing him, was crushing. She'd do anything to avoid hurting him, but she had to be upfront about her decision so he could get on with appointing the next head groom.

When it came to writing a formal letter of resignation, which would have to follow the text, however long it took to arrive, she ended up scrapping three attempts. Tears spoiled the rest. Raffa meant everything to her. He'd been an exceptional boss. She'd learned so much from him. The chance to work with his top-class horses was a gift she would never be able to repay, but the faster she could get the animal therapy courses up and running at Sofia's new retreat, the sooner she'd have something concrete to offer her father.

And Raffa?

Dreams should be confined to childhood where they could do no harm, Rose concluded as she bit down on her kiss-swollen lips.

'Raffa!' She jolted upright as the door flew open. Glorious and powerful, he was also absolutely steaming mad. Gathering her scattered wits, she stood to confront him. 'Did you forget something?'

Ignoring the question, he held out his phone. 'What is the meaning of this?'

'So you've read my text.'

'D'you think?'

Skirting around him, she closed the door he'd left open. When she turned back, he was facing the fire. She didn't need to see his expression to read the tension in his back. How could she explain to a man as driven as Raffa Acosta that loyalty was as complex as love, and that Rose's duty lay with her father because he couldn't help himself?

He swung around abruptly. 'Well? Would you care to explain your text?'

His unwavering stare held her in check for a moment, but she rallied fast. 'It's only fair to you and my colleagues to give someone else the chance to be Head Groom.'

'What about your chance, Rose?'

'I can look after myself.'

His expression darkened. 'And is this what you really want?'

'It's not what I want,' she tried to explain, 'but it's what's possible.'

'So, you're determined to stay on in Ireland. And do what?'

'Work for your sister.'

Raffa couldn't have looked more shocked. 'You're going to work for Sofia?'

'It's the only answer,' Rose insisted. 'My father needs me. I must stay here. I have to earn money.

How else can we live? Even if I have to stand alone on this, I'm rejecting your offer to buy the farm. I'll find another way—talk my brothers around—'

'Your father needs professional help,' Raffa interrupted, 'which will be more effective if he's left to focus on his therapy for a while. I need you in Spain to fulfil the contract you signed—the contract I countersigned in good faith. Do you even have a plan going forward?'

'Yes, of course I have a plan.' She could only hope it wouldn't shatter when she put it out there, as the warmth, trust and openness she'd shared with Raffa had. 'I'm going to run animal therapy sessions at your sister's retreats, beginning with the one in Ireland.'

'Nice of you to discuss this with me first.' Raffa's sarcasm was more cutting than the coldness on his face. 'Does our recent past mean nothing to you?'

'Of course it does.'

The words were ripped from her soul, but Raffa remained unconvinced. 'Is this you being stubborn?' he demanded, frowning. 'Because surely you can see that you stand to lose more than you gain.'

'I'm not trying to gain anything,' Rose attempted to explain. 'I'm trying to help.'

'You're not getting back at me for my "buying spree" in the village, as Sofia puts it?'

'I would never be so petty,' she defended hotly.

Raffa exhaled slowly. 'I need you, Rose,' he admitted grimly. 'My ranch needs you.'

'You can easily find another head groom.'

'Not like you. Your father and brothers don't need you to oversee their every move. You're finally free, Rose. Can't you see that?'

'I must see my father settled.'

'Are you creating work for yourself? Or are you too frightened to come back to Spain?'

'Frightened?' Rose asked with surprise. 'I apologise for firing off that text without proper thought, but I won't change my mind. My father has this one chance, and, with your help and Sofia's, I hope things will improve for him. Only then can I consider what I want to do.'

'What do you want, Rose?'

She frowned as she thought about it. 'The chance to be me, I suppose.'

'You've got that chance now,' Raffa said fiercely. 'Why don't you take it?'

Rose slowly shook her head. 'I know I've hurt you, but I could never have predicted how quickly my father's condition would descend into violence.'

'Given your father's volatility, you must have known from the start that accepting a position on my ranch held a degree of risk, but you took that job with all it entails. I don't accept your resignation. You're a courageous woman, Rose, but you still have to learn that it takes more courage to step forward than back.'

Raffa's words echoed in Rose's head long after he'd slammed the door behind him. Was she destined to spend the rest of her life frightened that love might leave as it had when her mother died? Raffa was so special, was the thought that he might live up to his formidable reputation and walk away holding her back? He was doing everything in his power to help her. Why was she ranging herself against him? Was he right in saying she was holding on to a cause that no longer needed her? If that was true, it could only be to avoid the risk of breaking her heart.

He hammered the gas all the way back to the pub. Rose was strong enough to make her own decisions. If they excluded him, so be it. No woman had ever put so many obstacles in his way, but easy was boring. He was always seeking new challenges, but he hadn't expected one to come in the form of a woman who checked him every step of the way.

Springing down from the vehicle straight into a pothole of mud, he cursed in a variety of languages, but ended up laughing at yet another example of how Rose could distract him beyond reason. It made no sense to keep her close when she was determined to follow her own path, but what had common sense ever had to do with him and Rose? Each time he brought logic into play where Rose Kelly was concerned, logic let him down.

The silence was deafening. She'd heard nothing from Raffa in the week since their last encounter at the farm, but she'd thought about him night and day, wishing she'd left the door open instead of sending that text, and then compounding it by insisting she intended to follow her own path. Even the progress she'd made with drawing up plans for the animal therapy programmes couldn't close the yawning gap left by a man with expressive black eyes and a will as strong as her own.

Was this love?

No, this was pig-headed stubbornness. That was what it was. So, suck it up, Rose. She was ready to fire the starting gun on recruiting staff and identifying animals for the Irish retreat—there were others who could do that, but Rose must oversee it.

Must she? Did she execute every job on the ranch, or were others quite capable of handling things on their own without her close supervision? Wasn't the idea of a team just that—each part knew what it had to do and got on with it?

With a growl of frustration—who liked to hear the truth, especially when it came from herself?—Rose picked up the phone to confirm with the applicants she'd chosen that the status of the project was full steam ahead.

There was still the achingly hollow hole left by Raffa. If Rose had thought distance would soothe her where that was concerned, she was wrong. He might have ignored her letter of resignation, but the urge to share every tiny detail of the progress at the retreat with him was eating away at her. There were some things he did know. Raffa had visited her father, which had shocked Rose to the core. Facing up to the truth, that she was no longer the crucial element without which her family would crumble, left her feeling calmer, and ready to speak to Raffa. It was long past time to talk things through with him face to face.

'He's not here, love,' Sylvia, the landlady at the pub, informed Rose. 'I thought he would have let you know that he flew back to Spain this morning.'

'Right. Yes.' Having anticipated a rational discussion with Raffa, Rose was completely thrown. She puckered her brow as if recollecting. 'I must have got the days mixed up.'

She trembled all the way home—from shock at Raffa's leaving. There was nothing to be done about it, she told herself fiercely. Lifting her chin, she strode on.

There was a parcel waiting for her at the farmhouse. Rose's heart turned over when she identified Raffa's bold black script. Backing into the kitchen, tearing the package open as she went, she pulled out the note inside.

Thought you might need this. R

It was the notebook Rose had been keeping since the day she started work on Rancho Raffa Acosta. It was thoughtful of Raffa to send it on, but it felt like the first step in a long goodbye. She guessed it had been found on the jet and one of his people had sent it back to him. Rose was never careless with things like this, and had to accept that a world full of Raffa

Acosta was a world full of distraction. Turning the notebook over in her hand, she imagined him thinking about her as he sent it on, maybe hoping she took it as a sign to move on.

That was what she wanted, wasn't it?

Then why did she feel so bad?

A few days later another delivery arrived from Raffa. She didn't open this one right away. Instead, she placed it on the kitchen table, where it sat like a silent visitor, waiting to be acknowledged. The packaging was neat, the handwriting unmistakeable. What was it this time? A scold's bridle to stop Rose speaking her mind, or maybe a potion for removing mud from her clothes? She braced herself for hurt as she glanced at it. Still, it was thrilling to know Raffa was still thinking about her—in a purely professional sense, of course. He was noted for his concern for staff members.

Walking around the table, she trailed her fingertips over the packaging, imagining him holding it, lifting it, writing her name. Sitting down at the table, she finally reached out to grab it and rip off the paper. It was an academic book on the study of animals and their great value in helping those with addictions. What broke her was seeing the name on the spine. Having met the author on board the *Pegasus*, and admired his work, Raffa had given her the most precious gift possible. She hugged it close, as if that could transmit her gratitude. Then she read the message on the flyleaf.

Thought you might need this too. R

If this was Raffa's blessing for Rose to go her own way, it was the most thoughtful goodbye she could think of. There was no reason to feel sad. So why was she crying? What good were tears when there was work to be done? Her first job was to thank Raffa for the gift. Finding paper and pen, she took a moment to think, then wrote.

Thank you for such a thoughtful gift. I will need this.

I need you too. She didn't write that bit down.

Please tell the professor I'll treasure every word.

Another pause followed and then she wrote more.

Until we meet again. R

She was effectively saying goodbye to her dream, a dream that had changed beyond all recognition when she became emotionally and physically involved with Raffa.

Had that dream changed? Was she incapable of compartmentalising work and romance? She didn't exactly sit around daydreaming on hay bales, or waste time in bed, discussing the respective merits of various horse liniments.

Too much time had been spent worrying about

planning and logistics, Rose concluded. Could she do this or that, while she was here or there? What about risking her heart for a change?

CHAPTER ELEVEN

'A CALL FROM ROSE? Put it through.'

A slow breath pealed out of him when he heard the familiar voice. It was like a cooling draught in an overheated desert, where playing polo for his friend the Sheikh was more of an endurance test than a pleasure. Propping his hip against an ornate gilded console table, Raffa longed for the simplicity of Rose's kitchen. He'd just kicked off his boots, after returning to his opulent, air-conditioned suite in the Sheikh's palace to shower and dress for dinner. But speaking to Rose was far more important than donning a tux.

'Are you okay? Is something wrong? Do you need help, Rose? Money?'

'I'm fine, Raffa. Honestly. I just wanted to thank you for the package you sent.'

'It was nothing.'

'It was everything to me,' Rose argued firmly. 'I learned so much from my short time with the professor, and to think you went to the trouble of getting hold of a signed copy of his book with that lovely message, saying our chat was the highlight of his evening. Of course it's important to me. I'll treasure it.'

Silence could be as intimate as speech, he discovered. He'd discovered a lot of things with Rose. Neither of them rushed to break that silence as he remembered how pleased he'd been to see a professor he respected deep in conversation with Rose.

'I'm sorry if I've kept you from your work.'

'You haven't,' he assured her. 'Are you sure you're okay?'

'Honestly, Raffa, don't worry about me.'

Someone had to. He pictured Rose and dragged in a breath, as if the air around him carried her wildflower scent. 'Are you busy?' he asked, wanting to keep her on the line.

'Yeah.' She laughed. 'Mucking out.' There was a pause, and when he laughed, she added, 'Did I say something funny?'

Apart from the fact that he had to get it through his head that Rose was no shrinking violet, or precious princess, but a stand-up woman who was almost certainly leaning on a pitchfork surrounded by dung. 'Mucking out?' he repeated. 'Can't you find someone to do that for you?'

'Why should I?' Rose sounded perplexed. 'No one makes my horses more comfortable than me. They've missed me while I've been away, haven't you?'

He recalled the ancient ponies on her farm, and wondered if Rose would use them for the animal therapy project. Almost certainly, he concluded. Rose thought of everything for everyone, including her horses. The old-timers would love nothing more than having renewed an interest in their lives.

'I really have to go now,' she apologised. 'These babies are waiting to be fed—'

'You called me,' he reminded Rose, frowning. Why would she do that, unless she had something more important to say than thank you? 'Rose?' He stared at the dead receiver in his hand. They knew each other well enough for him to know when she was holding back. But why? Was it because whatever Rose had wanted to say couldn't be said over the phone?

Concern leapt inside him. What was going on?

He called his sister, who confirmed his concern was well founded. 'Rose is working all hours, trying to do everything herself. She won't listen to me,' Sofia told him with concern. 'It's as if she's in a race to get everything in place for her father. I've never known anyone to work so hard. She needs you to slow her down, Raffa. You're the only one she'll listen to—'

He'd heard enough. His next call was to the Sheikh. Making his apologies on the basis of an urgent family matter, he booked a flight plan to Killarney and Rose.

Rose was in the middle of interviewing potential staff for the new retreat when Raffa appeared at the door. Surprise shot her out of her seat. 'Your timing is terrible.'

'My timing, as always, is impeccable,' Raffa argued with a long, assessing look. 'I've sent the candidates for lunch, so you can take a break. Have you eaten anything today?'

Rose's heart started thudding. Raffa was taking control again. 'You had no right to dismiss the applicants. I plan to eat as soon as I finish the interviews.'

'You look tired, Rose.'

'I'm not tired,' she fired back. 'Aren't I allowed to be surprised to see you? If I'd known you were coming—'

'You'd have made yourself scarce?' he suggested dryly.

'I would have carried on as usual,' she insisted, straightening up, 'but with a bigger break so we'd have a chance to talk. As it is?' She shrugged. 'I can't spare the time.'

Ignoring that, he scanned the room. 'Is this your bag?'

'Yes,' she said hesitantly. 'What's this leading up to?'

'You might want to bring it with you. My assistant will continue the interviews, leaving you free for the rest of the day—' He held up his hand when Rose began to interrupt. 'The man taking over from you is Sofia's trusted colleague. It was Sofia herself who—'

'Sent in an enforcer?' Rose suggested with an accusatory look.

He ignored that too. 'When did you last eat or sleep? And don't tell me you're fine. I can see the exhaustion in your eyes. I'm here to help, Rose. I have resources. Use them. Allow others to pick up the slack before you fall asleep on the job.'

'I can't just walk out of here,' she protested.

'Why not? Delegate the rest of your work, and come back stronger and fresher.'

A wave of tiredness hit, making Rose sway in her seat. Just the mention of taking a break was so tempting. As was the concern in Raffa's eyes. She couldn't take much more of caring Raffa, before she ugly-sobbed and clung to him. And he did have a point. The retreat was well on its way to completion. They'd open soon, which would allow Rose to pull back from devoting every waking hour and most of the night to the project.

'Ready?' he asked from the door.

'This won't take long, will it?' she asked, imagining a quick bite at the pub.

'That depends on how long you're going to take.'

The hint of a smile on Raffa's face drew her out of the seat like a magnet. 'I suppose I can take my lunch hour now.'

'No suppose about it,' he insisted.

But they didn't stop at the pub. He took her in the car—she thought they were going to the Old Hall, to take a look at how things were going on. He drove straight past, continuing on to a destination unknown. 'Where are we going?' She glanced around as she sifted through the various possibilities in her mind.

'To Spain,' Raffa said casually.

'What? I can't go to Spain! I'm needed here.'

'If I leave you here,' he said calmly, 'you'll collapse with exhaustion. Thanks to your hard work the opening of the retreat has been brought forward. I see no reason why you can't supervise the rest of the project remotely, as I do with many of my business concerns. Your father's in safekeeping until he takes up his place at my sister's retreat in Ireland, so there's no reason why you can't take a break. I can't be sure you'll do that, unless you come home with me.'

Home. Home with Raffa? Rose glanced around. 'This is my home,' she protested.

'You can't have two homes? You can supervise the therapy programmes remotely. Come back for a rest. Give yourself a chance to think clearly.'

If she was honest, for once in her life she was almost glad to be offered the chance to take a breath. 'So, I shouldn't worry about you trying to control me?'

Raffa huffed a laugh at that. 'I control my work and my horses. I have zero desire to control you—that's even if I could, which, I'm happy to say, I can't. I wouldn't change a thing about you—apart from your stubbornness when it comes to refusing to think about yourself.'

He wanted the best for Rose. Having seen her so free in his arms, he wanted her free all the time. She was working herself to death, trying to save everyone and everything, when it was as clear as day that what Rose needed was saving from herself.

'The airstrip,' she exclaimed as they passed through the gates. 'But my letter of resignation's in the post.'

'So? I haven't read it yet,' he said with a shrug. Nor would he. 'This isn't about work, Rose. It's about you taking a well-earned rest.'

She gave him one of her looks. 'You have to kidnap me to make me rest?'

'Appears so,' he agreed.

The look on Rose's face pierced his heart in a

thousand different places. She was too tired to think straight, but his thoughts were all in order. 'I want you back, Rose. You don't belong behind a desk, organising schedules.'

'There's a lot more to my job at the retreat than scheduling.'

'Training therapists?' he suggested. 'Trying to pass on the fairy dust that makes you so special? Come on, Rose, you're a hands-on woman with exceptional skills. Are you happy to throw all that away?'

Rose couldn't pretend she didn't have doubts about the direction her career was taking. Once she'd set up the therapy programme there'd be very little hands-on work for her to do. Was it the loss of control or the loss of Raffa that was turning her upside down? There'd been no controlling her father in one of his rages. Had that left its mark? Was Raffa trying to control her, or was he trying to help?

'You don't have to devote every waking moment to work,' Raffa insisted.

'Says you, who's mired in work,' she pointed out.

'I would never stop you leaving if you got a better offer, though I'd fight like hell to keep you—'

As his head groom?

Of course as his head groom. What more did she expect?

She didn't want that to be her future. What Rose longed for more than anything was a proper work-life balance, and for that balance to include Raffa on both sides of the equation. She just didn't know how to achieve it. Work had always been her safe space that allowed her to shut out everything else—the arguments at home, and the grief at the loss of her mother, and then, more recently, her ever deepening feelings for Raffa.

'I'll do anything I can to stop you making a fatal mistake,' Raffa insisted as he swung the wheel to bring the SUV to a standstill at the steps of the Acosta jet. 'But I refuse to stand by and watch you take a disastrous path that can only lead to a dead end. I know your potential, Rose, and I can't let you squander it. Your father's future is secure. What he needs now is space, so the professionals have the chance to help him. He's at a stage where guilt is his main enemy, which is why it's important for him to know that you have a life too.'

Rose exhaled and shook her head. 'You know just which buttons to press.'

'I have no ulterior motive here. I'm simply being honest with you, Rose. It's time for you to let go. It's your turn to fly.'

'Taking my foot off the pedal at work doesn't come naturally,' she admitted, wondering if they were still talking about work. Was this polo superstar Raffa Acosta making his bid for the woman he believed was the best head groom, or was Raffa asking Rose to stay for another reason? This wasn't a movie with a happy-ever-after ending guaranteed. Life was tougher than that.

Yes, Rose's inner critic agreed, for once. When you want something, you have to go for it. You have to take risks—not all of them calculated. Sometimes it's necessary to act on pure instinct.

And if that means returning to Spain?

Raffa hadn't made a fortune in tech only to live in the Dark Ages. She could still be in touch with her father's therapists and with the programmes at the retreat, as well as with her brothers and anyone else Rose needed to contact. There was actually no excuse for her to stay behind in Ireland. She could work anywhere in the world and still keep her foot on the pedal. But there was something to sort out first. 'Even after a letter of resignation, you'd have me back?'

'What letter of resignation?'

When he stared at her like that, Rose knew exactly what she had to do.

CHAPTER TWELVE

ROSE SETTLED STRAIGHT back into life on the ranch.
After a week of rest, during which Adena took over as
Head Groom, Rose began to feel refreshed. Sleeping
late, and eating her fill of the delicious food on offer,
together with swimming in the river when she wasn't
riding flat out through the lush green meadows with
the wind in her hair, all contributed to her growing
sense of peace. There was only one thing missing, and
that was Raffa, who'd said she needed space.

Not this much space, Rose reflected as she paced
the office he'd set aside for her. It wasn't all bad. Máire
had contacted Rose out of the blue to say she'd like to
be involved in the new retreat. Working with friends
was a gift Rose had found on the ranch, and she was
thrilled to think it could continue in Ireland.

Her thoughts returned to Raffa and she sighed,
missing everything about him—the chat, the laughter, the banter they'd shared, as well as their closeness.
At least she could concentrate on work while he was
away. Well, that was the theory, until she left the office
to go to the tack room, where she found her friends

clustered around the TV. The feature they were watching showcased a man who lit up the screen.

'Romance?' Raffa was querying in answer to one of the reporter's questions. 'Romance is for those with too much time on their hands.'

Rose flinched.

'So, you're not a romantic person?' the reporter stubbornly persisted to a background of Raffa and Rose dancing at Sofia's wedding.

'I'm a practical man who believes in chivalry,' Raffa said with a shrug. 'An outdated quality, no doubt—'

'Would your groom have dared to refuse you?' the young woman interrupted with a simpering laugh.

'The person in question knows where to draw the line—something I suggest you embrace.' Ripping off his microphone was the producer's cue to cut quickly to Raffa whacking a ball across a polo field with the force of a bullet to a chorus of good-natured cheers from the tack room.

'With all that talk of chivalry, he does belong in another era,' one of the young male grooms proposed, with a cheeky sideways glance at Rose. 'When men were men and women did what they were told,' he added recklessly, to the accompaniment of a bucket full of pony nuts being tipped over his head by Adena.

While chaos ensued, Rose watched a montage of Raffa on the screen. He hadn't needed her on this business trip, as he'd only played one match. Her heart ached with longing. No amount of common sense could deal with that. The camera loved him. She loved

him, and it was getting harder by the day to hide that
fact from her friends.

'There's a letter for you, Rose,' Adena announced
as the good-natured scrum in the tack room broke up,
and everyone returned to their duties. 'I recognise the
handwriting. I wonder what it is this time.'

Since the day Raffa had embarked on this latest
trip, he'd been in contact with Rose constantly, not
on a romantic level, of course, for which, if she had
an iota of that common sense she was supposedly famous for, she should be grateful.

She was not grateful. She missed him like hell.
Each delivery had contained something practical connected to her job. If there was ever a signal that it was
time for Rose Kelly to get real and finally accept that
Raffa Acosta had no wish to embark on a long-term
relationship with his head groom, then surely, that was
it? Shutting off the screen, she blanked her mind to
every taut and tanned muscle.

'Aren't you going to open the letter?' Adena pressed.

'Not here.' Rose smiled apologetically. She craved
the privacy of her room. 'It's probably just a list of in-
structions to add to those I already have,' she said as
she tucked the envelope into her pocket.

Once her door was closed, she ripped the envelope
open. And gasped. It was an invitation to spend her
birthday on board Raffa's superyacht.

As fast as surprise and elation swept over her,
gloom set in. The accompanying note was hardly romantic.

*This will be an ideal chance to discuss business.
I'm inviting some people I'd like you to meet. R*

'That sounds like fun,' Rose murmured, pulling
a face.

But why not? Why the hell not? Socialising was part
of her job, and for as long as it lasted she'd do that job
to the very best of her ability. And if she didn't wear
those fabulous clothes hanging in her dressing room
on board the *Pegasus*, who would?

Don't even go there, Rose's inner critic advised.
Just reply to the invitation and accept.

Raffa sent a helicopter to the ranch to pick her up. As
it hovered overhead Rose hoped with all her heart he'd
be at the controls. He wasn't. A cordial older man in
uniform came to help her board. There was scarcely
any conversation on the way, bar the information that
they would be joining the *Pegasus* off the coast of
Spain. Would Raffa greet her when they arrived, or
would he be too busy? He might not even be on board,
she reasoned sensibly. Helicopters were nifty taxis for
the super-rich. He could be anywhere.

With anyone.

And that was none of her business.

How could her heart be so wrong? Rose wondered
as the pilot helped her down on to the deserted deck.
No welcoming committee this time. Just the instruction to report to the grand salon. Thankfully, the sea
was smooth today with just the slightest hint that the

ground was shifting beneath her feet. How apt, she thought as she opened the doors to the grand salon.

'*Surprise!*'

She gasped with shock. There were banners everywhere, wishing Rose a happy birthday, and so many people she knew—some she hadn't seen for ages. *And all her brothers!*

'How—'

Sofia was at her side in moments. 'Come with me.' Raffa's sister linked arms with Rose to draw her deeper into the crowd. 'You deserve this,' she shouted above the cheers, as Rose shook her head in bewilderment. 'This is our chance to say thank you, for all your hard work on the new retreat, for the programmes you set up and for…well, just being you.'

'I don't know what to say,' Rose shouted back.

'You're going to enjoy this,' Sofia promised. 'Kellys *and* Acostas, as well as a prince or two. If that isn't a chilli-spiked mix, I don't know what is. I'm a respectable married woman, but even I'd have to be wood from the neck up not to think lock up your daughters when the Kelly brothers are here.'

'I can't believe they're all here,' Rose marvelled. 'How on earth did you find them?'

'Thank Raffa, not me,' Sofia explained. 'There isn't a thing that man can't do when he puts his mind to it. And don't mind your brothers—look at the cake!'

A snowy white damask tablecloth set off a towering edifice of chocolate and cream. 'Six entire feet of chocolate heaven,' Sofia enthused. 'I can't wait for you to cut into it.'

Rose stared ruefully at her rumpled travelling clothes. 'I'm not dressed for this.'

'None of us are, but we will be,' Sofia promised.

'Happy birthday, Rose...'

The familiar deep husky tone thrilled its way through Rose's body. Raffa's eyes finished the job. His expression was such a mix of brooding purpose and delicious promise, her words came out jumbled and all in a rush. 'Just seeing my brothers again—I can't express—I don't deserve this.'

'Sofia assures me you do. Please accept this as our birthday gift. Can I interest you in a glass of champagne?'

'Oh, no, I should keep a clear head, but thank you. I imagine there are people you want me to meet.'

'You do as you please tonight. This is your birthday party.'

'I'd like to say hello to my brothers.'

'What are you waiting for?'

She glanced up, thanks blazing in her eyes. The last time she'd had a birthday party her mother had been alive.

Rose, Rose, Rose, Raffa reflected, thumbing his stubble as he watched Rose's exuberant reunion with her brothers. Everyone enjoyed spending time with Rose. The entire impossible-to-please Acosta clan appreciated what Rose had accomplished, both on his ranch, where she had improved rotas and training regimes, and at Sofia's retreats, where her programmes were already making a difference.

And then there were his personal feelings for Rose.

If he'd been a different man, things might have moved faster with Rose, but protecting her from his darkness took priority. That said, it was becoming harder each day to be apart from her. Imagining Rose with another man was totally unthinkable.

'I've got an announcement to make,' Sofia declared in her usual fizzy tone as she tapped on a glass. 'Your Royal Highnesses, lords, ladies and gentlemen—'

He might have known several jokers would insist there were no gentlemen present.

'To honour our friend Rose Kelly,' Sofia continued the moment order had been resumed, 'we're going to take a short break to get changed into our finery. And no shenanigans while you're below decks,' she warned with a mischievous twinkle, 'or the party will never get started.'

This remark brought about a fresh bout of good-natured laughter, during which Raffa asked the purser to make sure a steward accompanied Rose to her suite. He was determined she would feel at home on the *Pegasus*, not as his employee, but as a valued friend of the family.

Closing the door on the now familiar sumptuous accommodation, Rose rested back against the wood with relief. She needed a few quiet moments to get her head around everything that had happened in the past few hours. The birthday party was such a lovely thing for Raffa and Sofia to have arranged, but Raffa's appraising stare had told her nothing beyond his concern.

Trying to be businesslike and sensible about this, she reasoned, pulling away from the door, was impossible where Raffa was concerned, when just seeing him again was enough to flood her mind with images of his impossibly powerful body pressing hungrily against hers.

Heading for the dressing room to pick out something to wear for the party, she wanted to impress him. What was wrong with that? Today was her birthday, and this year she was gifting herself Raffa.

He was as stunned as everyone else when Rose returned to the party. Bathed in moonlight, she looked like an old-time movie star in a slim column of night-blue silk, with a split up the side that revealed her flawless legs. But, once again, it was her hair that took the prize. She had chosen to wear it loose, and it tumbled to her waist in a fiery profusion of shimmering waves. Lust fired inside him. Rose Kelly fired him in every way possible. There were many beautiful women on board the *Pegasus* tonight, but none compared to Rose, because her inner beauty, fired by a generous heart and a loving nature, meant she could not be outshone.

'Will you dance with me, *señorita*?' he asked, bowing over Rose's hand, marvelling at how pale and slim it was, and yet how strong.

'I'd love to,' she said in her customary unaffected way.

Rose's delectable scent and quick smile intoxicated him, as did the sparkle of challenge in her bright emerald eyes. This promised to be an outstanding evening.

'You dance well, *señorita*,' he said, relishing the brush of her body against his.

'I have an excellent partner,' she replied with a grin and the lift of a brow.

Rose might be in the mood for teasing him, but tonight she looked like a queen—a queen who moved in his arms as if she belonged there. The acid stares from her brothers suggested the attraction between them was glaringly obvious. Don't hurt her, their looks said, as clearly as if Rose's brothers had bellowed the instruction in his ear.

'What can we do about this?' he reflected out loud.

'About what?' Rose asked.

Sweeping her brothers' concern from his mind, he voiced his own. 'I haven't got a birthday gift for you.'

'What's this?' Rose demanded, glancing around. 'Isn't this party the most wonderful gift? Not to mention the gown I'm wearing,' she added, smoothing an appreciative hand over the tailoring.

'These are such small things, Rose.'

'Not for me,' she assured him with a reproachful look.

At a loss to know how to please a woman who expected nothing from him, when he wanted to do so much for her, he drew Rose close again and they danced on. But not for long. 'I really should go and look after the guests,' she told him during a brief pause in the music. 'My brothers will never forgive me if I don't introduce them around.'

And with that she was gone. He filled the gap left by Rose by making sure everyone was enjoying themselves. They caught up later at the cake table, where Rose, surrounded by a crowd of well-wishers, was telling everyone that she'd been spoiled tonight.

'No more than you deserve.'

She turned at the sound of his voice. 'Raffa!' Her glowing eyes told him everything he wanted to know, and he was glad when her companions took the hint and melted away.

'This is such an amazing night,' she enthused. 'Just look at this cake…'

The lightest touch of Rose's hand on his arm was a thunderbolt to his senses. He followed her stare to the towering mountain of chocolate icing, festooned with various horse-related candies attached to each layer of the mammoth structure. On the topmost layer, the figure of a woman riding a horse was supposed to represent Rose, but the sculpted hair on the marzipan figurine was bright orange, while the horse was a dull, chocolatey brown. Neither did justice to Rose, or to her favourite pony. It was a good attempt by his chef, but now he wished he'd sent for a master patissier from Paris. The hair should be glittering gold, and the pony should have its ears pricked and its head turned towards Rose.

The ceremony of cutting the cake was a welcome break from the growing sexual tension between them. Rose made a big play of wielding the knife in a way that made everyone laugh, but then she grew serious and made a short speech. Thanking both him and Sofia, for the opportunities they'd put her way, as well as the chances they'd given to so many more people, she also thanked her guests for taking valuable time out of busy schedules to join the celebration.

'There's no one more deserving than you,' his sister called out.

Sofia's comment was received by answering cheers as Rose cut the cake. He took a glass of champagne to Rose so they could toast her birthday. 'You still haven't told me what you'd like for a gift,' he reminded her.

'Being here with my family and friends is enough,' she assured him.

'Some small token, surely?' he pressed.

She thought about it for a moment, then held up the untouched glass of champagne in her hand. Like all the crystal on board the *Pegasus*, the image of a flying horse was etched on the side of the flute. 'How about this, so I can remember tonight forever?'

He pulled his head back with surprise. Even for a woman he knew could not be bought with riches, this was a disappointingly modest request. 'I'm sure I can think of something better than a champagne glass for you to remember tonight by.'

Her eyes filled with longing, but only for a moment, and then, Rose being Rose, she reverted to her usual cheeky self. 'You just don't want to break up a set,' she said, eyes dancing with amusement.

CHAPTER THIRTEEN

'BROODING?' ROSE ASKED Raffa towards the end of the evening.

A helicopter beating a noisy retreat overhead spared him the need to supply an answer. It would have been necessarily brief. If he couldn't explain to himself why his past failings still haunted him, or how he woke in the night, believing he'd effectively killed his parents, how could he put into words how he felt about Rose, or how he feared losing her, as he'd lost others he'd loved? Watching Rose's reunion with her brothers had brought it all back to him. Seeing his own brothers—some married now, and seemingly free of the past—had made him question whether he deserved that same level of freedom.

'Your guests are leaving,' Rose prompted. 'Shall I report to the helipad, or to the stern where the small boats are leaving?'

'You're not leaving,' he exclaimed with surprise. 'You're my guest.'

'That's why I plan to go back with the rest of your guests. This has been one of the best nights of my life. I don't know how to thank you.'

'By not thanking me,' he insisted, frowning. 'There's no need.'

'Raffa?'

'Yes?' He stared down, then tensed as Rose put a comforting hand on his.

'I'm happy to stay, if you're feeling…'

As she searched for an appropriate word—one that wouldn't cause offence, he guessed—he changed his mind about having her stay. It would only lead to more hurt for Rose. 'You should leave on the last tender.'

'At least you're not saying I must leave,' Rose qualified with a glint of humour in her eyes. 'Can I be honest with you, Raffa?'

'Of course,' he said stiffly.

'I don't think you should be alone tonight.'

He laughed as he made a dismissive gesture. 'Do you seriously think I'll be alone?'

She followed his glance around the still crowded deck. 'You know what I mean. Sometimes I think we're like two lost souls, grieving and hurting, then shrugging it off, which solves nothing. We heal nothing,' she stressed in a soft yet intense tone. 'If you and I don't talk to someone—and for me, I'd like that someone to be you—we'll never move on. Don't,' she begged when he began to disagree. Reaching up, she placed her fingertips against his mouth. 'Please don't say there's nothing wrong, or that you're fine. That's been my mantra for years now—for all the good it's done me.'

There was another long pause, and then he suggested, 'My study?'

* * *

The chance to share quiet time with Raffa was the only birthday gift Rose craved, but with each step closer to Raffa's study, she worried that by the time they arrived in the privacy of his room he'd have changed his mind about opening up. Keeping things locked inside him was such a habit, there was no easy way to start talking.

He switched on the light and closed the door behind them. 'Sit,' he invited, indicating an easy chair. She perched on the edge, while he crossed the Persian rug, with its long history and muted shades, to a spectacular glass unit where he kept his drinks. Pouring two generous measures of brandy, he offered one to Rose. She accepted the fine crystal balloon, but even the smell of the alcohol was enough to put her off. 'Do you think I could have a glass of water instead?'

'Of course. Don't drink the brandy if you don't want it.' Filling a tumbler with ice, he topped it up with pure spring water.

'Won't you sit too?' she asked, knowing this was the best chance she had to stop Raffa strapping on his guilt even tighter. No one liked to admit to an Achilles heel. How much harder must that be for a man like Raffa Acosta? She knew what haunted him, because she felt the same need to fiercely protect everything and everyone she cared about. 'I build barriers,' she admitted with a shrug. 'So do most people until they're sure of their ground.'

'What are you trying to say, Rose?'

'That I understand you.' She paused. 'I respect you.

You're a great boss, and, of course, I want to have everything—my job with you, my place in Ireland and more besides…'

'What more besides?' he demanded, frowning.

'Don't you know?'

'If you insist on talking in riddles, I'll never find out.'

As he began to pace the room, she took the chance to open up a little more, in the hope of encouraging Raffa to do the same. 'The past made me afraid to show my feelings—afraid to risk my heart. I thought I couldn't live through the pain of losing my mother, and decided it was better not to feel anything ever again. Now I realise that nothing can erase the past, so I think of the good times—the fun we had—baking together, the laughter and charades at Christmas before she became sick. When I confronted the alternative, which was to stay home with a drunken father, getting nowhere, doing nothing, I finally came to terms with my mother's death, and realised that what she'd wanted for me was not to stay home and take her place, but to assume a moral responsibility for the family, so I could keep her purposeful, upbeat spirit alive. But to do that meant leaving home, so I could make enough money to keep things afloat.'

'You can see that now,' Raffa interjected. 'But you're just as guilty of beating yourself up. Deathbed promises can be misleading, and it's only natural you worry about letting your mother down.'

'That hasn't changed,' she admitted, 'but I'm equally sure your parents wouldn't expect you to hold yourself responsible for their deaths. Forgive me, Raffa,' she added gently. 'I don't want to step on your grief, I'm just trying to say, in my rather clumsy way, that we're fighting the same demons, you and I.'

Raffa remained silent for so long, she began to wonder if it was a hint for her to leave. She decided to test the theory. 'I apologise if I've overstepped the mark tonight. After such a great party, I should keep my mouth shut, and only open it to say thank you.'

Raffa's short, humourless huff wasn't much, but it was a start, and Rose clung on to it with relief. 'Forgive my silence,' he said after a few more tense moments had passed. 'I haven't talked about my feelings to anyone. The shock of losing my parents was overwhelming. There was no chance for a last hug, or for me to tell them how much they meant to me.'

'There's never enough time for that.'

Another pause, and then he met her concerned stare head-on. 'You've never had a problem being forthright, have you, Rose?'

She smiled ruefully. 'Isn't that why you hired me?'

'I hired you because you're the best,' Raffa confessed with a shrug. 'There was nothing more to it than that, until…'

'Until?' she pressed.

'I don't like fate to notice those I care about.'

'Fate's pretty busy, and can't be mean all the time,' she countered in an attempt to lighten his mood.

'Trust you to put a positive spin on fate's intentions, Rose.'

'Whatever fate has in store for me, I'll cope. I'm here for you, if you need me, but if you've just brought

me here to say the sex is great, but you feel nothing
for me—'

'That is not why I brought you here.'

They stared at each other for a long moment, and
then crashed together, two powerful forces colliding.
There was no submission or mastery, and no holding back, either. There was only matching hunger
and equal need. Raffa swept his desk clear. Clothes
went flying everywhere. Nudging his way between
her thighs, he sank deep with a roar of satisfaction,
only equalled by Rose's cries of release. There was no
finesse, none needed. They strove with full concentration towards the next staggeringly intense release.
It wasn't once, twice or even three times that Rose's
rhythmical cries of pleasure echoed around Raffa's
study, until finally she lay utterly spent in his arms.

'Again?' he teased.

She dragged in some much-needed air. 'What do
you think?'

When they were quiet again, Raffa mused huskily,
'I only wish there were more time to spend with you.'

'So, you've no time for sailing on your yacht, or
having sex with me in your study?'

'You deserve more than that, Rose. As for the yacht?'
He gave a casual shrug. 'It's useful for business.'

'My bike's useful for getting to the village from the
farm, but I don't make it an excuse for living in the past.
I've seen you torment yourself, and I've felt the reper-
cussions. I understand you, because I spent years being
stoic, and thinking I could take it. And it was true to
some extent. I could take pretty much anything until

you came along and opened up a well of feeling inside me. But you helped me too, because now I know I'd rather feel and bleed and cry than remain numb and sensible. I'm hungry to experience life, with all its challenges, and learn every step of the way. And if I can eventually raise a family to do the same, I'll count that as the greatest achievement of my life.'

'I can't offer you what you hope for, Rose, and I won't take the risk of you being hurt.'

'Isn't that up to me?' she demanded, frowning. 'It sounds to me as if you've decided to take the easy option and quietly back away.'

'Quietly?' Raffa raked his hair. 'There'll be nothing quiet about it.'

'Then open up,' she challenged. 'Offload some of your guilt. You're always telling me to share the load. You won't be free from the past until you do the same.'

'I would never do anything to hurt you.'

'Coward!' she flung at him with frustration. 'What do you think you're doing now, if not hurting me? Why can't you be honest with both of us? You refuse to risk anything but your body, and that will never be enough for me. Am I wasting my time?' she demanded.

'Rose—'

She brushed his comforting arm away. 'Lots of people live busy lives and still find time for love. What I need is you, constant and unchanging, not holding back emotionally because you think you're going to hurt me. Let me decide about that. We find it easy to laugh together, and challenge each other, why can't we turn that into something deeper? I'm not made of rice paper. I won't break if we go at it hammer and tongs. I'll come back fighting. You know I will.'

Raffa inhaled and drew himself up. 'I decided some time back that I would never have a family, because I don't have the time a family deserves. I'm a busy man with global interests. No one benefits from being dragged from pillar to post across the world.'

'You have your yacht,' Rose pointed out with exasperation. 'You can take your family and your home with you. Why can't you adapt your life like everyone else? Haven't you seen your brothers do that?' Something flickered in Raffa's eyes that drove Rose to press on. 'Or are you just too damn selfish to compromise? I refuse to believe that. A man who cares so deeply for his siblings must, in some deep part of him, want to recreate that same sense of warmth and love.'

'Children deserve parents who have time to lavish affection on them,' he argued stiffly.

'The same affection you lavish on your horses?' Rose suggested. 'Are you saying you can find time to do that, but you won't be able to show your children that same level of attention?'

'Aren't you getting ahead of yourself, Rose?'

'Maybe I am,' she admitted. 'And maybe I don't care. You'll marry someone one day—if only to hang on your arm at events. I care about you, Raffa. Can't you see that?'

He shook his head slowly. 'I have responsibilities towards the people who work for me. The families that depend on my companies for their livelihoods. What will they do if I'm distracted by a family of my own? How can I possibly—'

'I don't know,' Rose flared, all out of patience. 'Why don't you ask your brothers? These excuses are weak. You'd find ways to make things work. Love *is* hard, and it can be cruel. It can hurt like nothing else, but when it's right, it's wonderful and transforming for those with sufficient courage to claim it.'

'Are you calling me a coward again?' Raffa said hotly.

'Where romantic love is concerned? Yes.' Maybe he wasn't the man she thought he was. Maybe the infamous Raffa Acosta was just too selfish to spare any part of himself. 'When I choose someone to spend the rest of my life with, it will be a man who shares everything with me, as I share everything with him— and on every level, not just sex. I don't want some big spender who can put on a show, but who balks at the small things that really matter.'

'Is that how you see me?'

He looked shocked. If Rose could have taken back her angry words, she would have done. Emotion so often prompted exaggeration, and right now she was drowning in the stuff. Heat flooded her face as she remembered the small, thoughtful packages Raffa had sent while they'd been apart, and then tonight, the wonderful birthday party. Maybe the fault wasn't all with him. Maybe she was guilty too.

'No,' she admitted. 'That's not how I see you. You're generous to a fault, and always thoughtful. I didn't mean to sound ungrateful—'

'I don't want you to be *grateful*,' he roared. 'I didn't throw tonight's party to impress you. I arranged it because I care about you.'

Raffa cared about her. Shouldn't that be enough? What was wrong with her? Did she have to try and spoil everything? The last thing she wanted was a fight. Why was she constantly building obstacles between them as fast as Raffa dismantled them? Would it be such a terrible thing to work for him *and* sleep with him?

Yes. Worse. It would be a disaster. When Raffa married, as one day he would, Rose would be left pressing her nose against the glass, and that would be the end of her. She'd have to leave her job, and then what would become of her father?

Turning her face away so he couldn't see her expression, she spoke in a false bright tone. 'Well, I'd better be going. I don't want to overstay my welcome. Don't worry about me getting back. I'm a seasoned campaigner when it comes to taking small boats to shore.'

'You'll do no such thing,' Raffa stated firmly. 'It will be more time efficient to fly back on the helicopter.'

He sounded as if he were solving a minor transport hitch for one of his employees. She'd asked for that— begged for it, by mentioning romantic love, when Raffa couldn't have made it clearer that that was the last thing he wanted.

She hugged herself close to hide the fact she was shivering as he called up the pilot, to warn him there'd be another flight tonight. Well done, Rose. She'd ruined a perfect evening. Perhaps Raffa was right to keep his feelings in check where she was concerned. Perhaps Rose should try doing the same thing herself. He was already scanning documents on his desk, so she couldn't see his expression, but she didn't need to see his face when the tension in his back told its own story. 'I'll say goodbye, then…'

Silence. 'Thank you again for a wonderful evening,' she tried again. 'I'll never forget it—'

'I'll never forget you. Rose—'

She almost jumped out of her skin when Raffa swung around. 'Go,' he prompted with a glance at the door. 'You don't want to be late for your lift.'

Moving restlessly on her cosy bed in her cosy room at the ranch, feeling anything but cosy, Rose knew she had no one to blame but herself. Thanks to Raffa, her birthday celebration had been perfect, and she had to go and spoil it, by trying too hard to unlock him, while selfishly holding back on her own feelings. She wouldn't know the extent of the damage she'd caused until he returned to the ranch. Waiting only made things worse. Why hadn't she thought to ask him when he'd be back?

The peal of the phone shook her out of her dismal thoughts, and in one of those rare cosmic moments, she knew who it was. 'Raffa?'

'I'll be home tomorrow.'

Home? He made it sound as if they lived together in an altogether conventional way. How nice would that be?

'Call a full meeting of grooms for tomorrow at mid-day in the stable block.'

She shot to attention immediately. 'Yes—' He didn't give her time to ask if he needed anything else, before cutting the line.

That was not a call from brooding Raffa, or sensual Raffa; that was a call from her boss. Well, at least she could get one thing right. She had a fantastic team. The stable block ran like a well-oiled machine. Noon tomorrow, they'd all be on parade.

Having delivered Raffa's message to the other grooms, she set about cleaning out the stables. The rhythmical application of a scrubbing brush was great for ordering her thoughts. She scrubbed harder than usual today. Having parted on such bad terms with Raffa, she'd do anything she could to restore some ease between them. His phone call hadn't been exactly reassuring on that point, but even hearing his voice was better than nothing. She was glad she'd handwritten a note to thank him for the party. Her mother would countenance nothing less. Some things from the past should be cherished, Rose had learned, while others were best discarded. It was just sorting out which was which that was the problem…a problem she and Raffa shared. It would be nice to sort that problem out together, but that was clearly a dream too far.

If she became his mistress, Rose's inner niggler insisted, she could still have a career, and advise on Sofia's projects. She'd be in a far better place to help her father with Raffa's private transport at her beck and call.

Sell her soul for a free ride on a private jet? No, thank you! She wanted more than jewels and a jet. She wanted Raffa's heart. If he still had one to give.

Dios! What was Rose Kelly doing to him? No woman had ever got under his skin like this before. He was piloting the helicopter from the *Pegasus* to his ranch, not even waiting long enough that morning to pack a bag, and all because of Rose. He'd called the meeting to arrange a rota to exchange staff between Ireland and Spain. Rose was crucial to both set-ups. He wanted her to be flexible and not feel trapped. Business was not the only reason he was returning to the ranch. Rose was the main reason. Rose, and the unfinished business between them.

As he hovered over his vast estate, snow-capped mountains glinted in the distance. A rip of adrenalin surged through his veins. The thrill never diminished. This was his kingdom, his passion, his life's work.

So you are capable of feeling emotion. You just don't want the inconvenience of anyone laying their emotional needs on you. Land just is. It doesn't answer back. Right?

He hummed thoughtfully. Landing smoothly, he released his harness. Instinct told him where she'd be.

He found Rose exactly where he'd expected to find her, in the stable talking quietly to one of his ponies. Standing in a beam of light, she looked otherworldly, sensual, lush, ravishingly beautiful. 'D'you mind if I join you?' he asked.

She started at the sound of his voice, but just as quickly recovered. Her eyes analysed his manner in an instant, and a slow smile lit up her face. 'Hello,' she whispered. 'Welcome back. Come on in. Be my guest.'

'Too kind,' he murmured wryly. 'How are things, Rose?'

Better now, her kind eyes told him, but there was a shadow behind Rose's eyes that spoke of something else. They'd parted badly. His fault. Wanting to protect Rose from himself was not going so well. As she began to detail everything he needed to know about the ponies, he let her continue for the sheer pleasure of watching her mouth form the words, when what he really wanted was for Rose to break off and fling her arms around him, tell him that she'd missed him. He wanted those capable, work-worn hands on him now.

This was agony, way beyond frustrating, Rose thought as she chattered away. All she wanted was to tell Raffa how much she'd missed him and loved him.

And suspected she might be pregnant with his baby?

No. Not that. Not now. Not yet. Let them have this moment first.

Rose was as regular as clockwork, never late... never two weeks late, as she'd realised last night. She'd rushed out first thing this morning and bought a pregnancy test to confirm or discount her suspicions, and would use it as soon as—

The pony standing between them in the stall stamped

its hooves as if impatient for them to get on with it. Forced to blank her mind to what might or might not be, she swooped down to collect up her grooming kit. Standing up brought her face to face—or, more accurately, face to chest—with Raffa.

He stared down. She stared up. He reached out first, but his fingertips only had to brush her skin for her to launch herself into his arms. Their kiss was fierce and reassuring. She wanted it to last forever, but her fellow grooms, reliable as always, chose that same moment to arrive.

'Wipe away those tears,' Raffa whispered against her mouth. 'Or they'll think I've sacked you.'

'You wouldn't dare,' she whispered back.

'Try me,' he challenged with a bone-melting smile.

They weren't healed, but this was a giant step in the right direction. To hear humour from Raffa made happiness surge through every part of her. They were back. He was back. *It* was back—the humour that connected them.

He'd need that sense of humour if she was pregnant.

He turned serious. 'Have you eaten yet?' he asked with concern.

'I will when I've finished my work—and then there's the meeting, don't forget.'

'You never finish work,' Raffa remarked dryly, 'and there's just enough time before the meeting—'

'To eat?' she queried. No. She thrilled, reading Raffa's expression.

'Leave that now,' he insisted.

Rose doubted anyone noticed them leaving. They

crossed the yard hand in hand, fingers entwined as they walked purposefully in the direction of the cook-house, and then on past the door.

CHAPTER FOURTEEN

SLAMMING THE RANCH-HOUSE door behind them, he turned and lifted Rose. She sprang up and wrapped her legs around his waist in the same instant. A few swift adjustments later, and they were joined. Relief overwhelmed him.

'More— Now— Harder,' Rose gasped as she clung to him.

He couldn't speak. His energies were employed elsewhere.

After their first noisy release, he carried her up the stairs to his bedroom. They were both laughing with relief as he lowered her on to the bed. 'What are you waiting for?' Rose asked.

'I'm drinking you in,' he admitted as he stared into emerald eyes bright with fire and laughter.

'Don't take too long,' she warned. 'Remember, we've got a meeting to go to.'

'Practical to the last. Before you say it, I know what you're going to say—that's why I hired you.'

Stripping off his clothes while Rose did the same, he pulled her into his arms on the bed. 'Did you take a shave this morning?' she asked, cupping his face in her hands. 'I could file my nails on that stubble.'

'You like it.' Statement, not question.

'You know I like it. I like you.'

'Only like me?'

'Do you deserve more than a like?' She gasped as he took her firmly and deeply. 'You most definitely do.'

'So?' he queried with amusement.

'So, don't you dare stop. Remember the meeting. Time's short.'

'Less time for speaking, then.' He smiled, loving Rose's nerve and her courage, and the fresh wildflower scent that was so unmistakeably hers.

'Whatever happens now, or in the future,' she told him when they were quiet again, 'I want you to know how I feel. I love you,' she said plainly, 'and that won't change, whatever you think of me. I hope my telling you this doesn't change anything?'

It changed everything. The look on Rose's face, the concern and the warmth, and the love, tinged with anxiety, touched something deep inside him. Reaching for her, he brought her close. Turned out, that was entirely the wrong thing to do.

'Don't pat me like your bloody pony!' she exclaimed, yanking herself free. 'I don't want your reassurance only for you to push me away in a few hours' time. I've told you how I feel about you. At least have the good manners to let me know how you feel about me.'

Rose sprang up. He did too. Passion ran high between them, as usual. There was never a time when Rose backed off. That was one of the things he admired most about her, but she seemed additionally driven today.

'Tell me,' she insisted fiercely. 'If I have the courage to lay my heart on the line, don't you think you should too? If you don't want me, you only have to say.'

'Of course I want you—' Only now did he realise quite how much. But what could he offer her? A heart of stone? A driven life? Constant travel? No respite? None of the simple things Rose longed for, like a family of her own. Bringing her into his arms, he kissed her and, to his unbounded relief, Rose kissed him back.

'Kiss me like you never want to let me go,' she whispered against his mouth.

He should be saving her from a man who, by his own admission, was incapable of giving Rose what she really needed, but instead he kissed her until no barrier on earth could keep them apart.

They fell back together on the bed, embracing as passionately as if they'd just invented sex. 'I've missed you so much,' Raffa admitted hoarsely. 'I never thought I'd feel this way about anyone.'

'I missed you too,' Rose confessed, arching her back in ecstasy as he took her again.

This time their lovemaking was slow and tender and deep. Raffa stared intently into her eyes as he took her with as much care as if she were made of the rice paper she'd teased him about.

'Don't wait for me,' he whispered. 'This is all for you.'

She rode the waves until they subsided, and then lay nestled in his arms, waiting for a sign from Raffa that she wasn't wasting her time loving him as much as she did. Could a man who'd made love to her as he just had feel nothing for her? He found words difficult, she reasoned. Rose had always been upfront with words and actions, but not everyone was the same. Each touch, breath and gentle consideration Raffa had shown for her pleasure had to mean something, didn't it?

She hated feeling so vulnerable, but being with Raffa had stripped her soul bare. Feeling more emotional than usual, as if there really was far more at stake, she remembered the pregnancy test in her bag. 'It's nearly time for the meeting. We should go—' Grabbing a throw, she headed for the bathroom with her bag. No doubt she appeared purposeful, but she was crying inside. Whatever the test showed, Raffa had been given every chance to tell her that he loved her, and he'd let that chance go.

Rose excused herself from the meeting early, looking pale. When she returned, Raffa noticed the change in her right away. 'Are you all right?' he asked as soon as their colleagues had left them. 'Rose?'

'I must have eaten something,' she fudged, avoiding his stare.

'Get the doctor to check you over.' There was a full medical team on-site. 'Now,' he prompted when Rose hesitated. 'I can't allow you near the horses if there's the slightest chance you're under par.'

'I'm not sick,' she flared, turning around to face him.

'How can you be sure?'

'Because I'm pregnant.' She let the silence hang

for a few moments, before adding, 'I took a test and it's positive.'

His logical mind accepted this calmly. They hadn't been exactly abstemious. Even using protection there was always a risk.

Rose's face betrayed nothing. It was as if all the progress she'd made in expressing herself freely had taken cover behind a protective shield. There was nothing to compare with a mother's instinct. Rose would protect that child above herself.

That was the logical side of things, but something else was happening that he couldn't ignore. Feelings were erupting inside him faster than he could control. He was going to be a father. His own father had been the most wonderful man, and Rose would be the most wonderful—

She broke into his thoughts. 'You don't have to say anything. I know this won't work for you.'

He held up his hand. 'Give me a chance to take it in. It isn't every day I get the news that I'm going to be a father.'

'I don't expect you to become involved,' she continued as if he hadn't spoken. 'I can handle this on my own. You made it clear from the start that this sort of thing isn't something you'd want to be part of, and I accept that—'

'This sort of thing?' he interrupted blankly. A lifetime of telling himself that he would never have a family—that he didn't deserve a family, after the way he'd stood helpless as his parents had perished—had been turned on its head, firing his thoughts in all directions at once. He could hardly keep track of what Rose was saying, for wondering why he hadn't declared his happiness right away. Why was he selfishly keeping these thoughts to himself? Was it because a man locked in some ridiculous eternal struggle with guilt believed he had nothing to offer a child?

'I'll do what every single mother does,' Rose was saying as he refocused. 'I'll keep on working and juggle my commitments. I still have some savings left—'

'Stop.' His command was fired by anger at himself. Surely, he was better than this? 'Why would you struggle when I can help you?'

'Is that you saying you want to take over? Because, if it is,' she warned, 'I'm telling you now that I won't let you control every aspect of this pregnancy. I won't join the mares in your breeding block to be cosseted and guarded for the duration. I'm a healthy woman who doesn't need to be smothered by expert attention. All I ask is to care for my child.'

'Who says you can't?' He was beginning to see his way through the maze. Rose needed more than reassurance, she needed proof that he would care for her, whatever her decision. 'I get that you're up in the air right now, with hormones racing, but please give yourself the chance to think things through calmly before you turn me down. There are consequences I'm not sure you've considered.'

'Like what?' Rose demanded defensively.

'Like the fact that you can't continue to work as you do—'

She paled. 'Are you firing me?'

'Of course not.' Her question had shocked him. 'But I must lay out the facts. You can't have close contact with my horses. This is a professional stable, housing spirited, highly bred and occasionally unpredictable animals. I'd be derelict in my duty as your employer if I allowed you to take any risks. Let alone the fact that my insurance won't cover you in your current condition.'

The effect of his speech appeared on Rose's face in tension lines and pallor. 'I hadn't thought about that,' she admitted quietly.

'Why would you? You haven't given yourself a chance to consider anything properly.'

She frowned. 'But I should have thought things through…'

'In the time it took from taking the test to now? Don't be so hard on yourself, Rose. This is as new to you as it is to me, but we'll find a way. We'll make this work with plans that suit both of us, and, more importantly, that secure our baby's future happiness.'

He meant every word to reassure her, but they seemed to have the opposite effect on her. It was a shock to see Rose, strong, resilient Rose, the woman who challenged him every step of the way, drop her face into her hands and cry.

Rose blundered out of the room, barely knowing where she was heading. How could she have overlooked something as vital as insurance cover? A policy for a pregnant woman working in a professional stable? She doubted such a thing even existed. Wrapping her arms protectively around her waist, she headed off down the road from the ranch to the vast acreage beyond. The urge to find space surrounded by nature was the only thing she could think of to soothe her mind. What she didn't want was Raffa outlining his cold-blooded plans. For once in her life, Rose Kelly, the biggest planner of them all, wanted something far more elusive and precious—Raffa's love, for their baby, for Rose and for the family she longed for. She longed to share this overwhelming joy with him. She'd wanted Raffa to pull her into his arms and say he was the happiest man alive.

Piercing bird calls drew Rose's gaze skywards. There were eagles in this part of Spain. She loved to see them wheeling and jousting, coming together only to fly apart again, before yielding to some mysterious force that brought them back to fly together.

Was that love?

Whatever it was, watching the magnificent birds calmed and healed her. Any child would be lucky to be brought up here, but Rose had many things to consider—her father, the family, the farm, the programmes for Sofia and the fact that she couldn't stay here indefinitely, watching from the wings, trying to explain to a child why its father wasn't around all that often.

They'd move forward with or without Raffa, Rose vowed silently. Like every single mother on the face of the earth, she'd find a way. Hadn't she taken care of her brothers since her mother died? She wasn't exactly a novice when it came to running a home.

She was about halfway back when she spotted a rider. Only one person rode as fast and fluidly bareback on such a highly bred horse. *Raffa.* Why was he coming after her?

Bringing his horse to a halt in front of her, he stared down at her face with concern. 'Come on,' he encouraged, holding out a hand. 'You can ride with me.'

'I thought you didn't want me near your horses?'

'Without me to keep you safe, that still holds fast.'

'Where are you heading?'

'To the river, so Duque can cool his heels while we talk.'

If he wanted to talk she wouldn't turn him down. Taking hold of his hand, she sprang up behind him on to the horse. 'Arms around my waist,' he said as they took off at a steady canter. The temptation to rest her face against his back made her sit up straighter than ever.

Raffa dismounted first and then lifted her into his arms. 'I was worried about you,' he admitted. 'You looked so pale. Thank goodness you look a lot better now.'

'The fresh air helps.' As did he. 'Don't worry, I'll stay on for a while to make sure Adena feels confident enough to take over from me, and I'll call Sofia. Babies are supremely portable, so—'

'And you, Rose?' Raffa interrupted. 'What about you?'

'Me?' She stared into his eyes. 'I'll be fine, of course.'

'Living where?'

'Here, in the short term, if you'll have me, and then I'll go back to Ireland, I suppose.'

Doubts crowded in, but if she couldn't work with Raffa's horses, there was nothing here for her. 'Maternity benefits will kick in eventually,' she reflected out loud.

'We have an excellent plan in place,' Raffa confirmed, 'but I don't see you resting as you should if you return to Ireland. When I brought you back to Spain, you were on the verge of exhaustion. A repeat of that would be dangerous, both for you and the baby.'

'I'll be sensible,' she promised.

'Until you have a thorough check-up, you don't know what is and isn't possible. Everyone's different, Rose. You're safer here.'

'Your mares carry some of the most valuable stock in the world, and you keep them in regal splendour, but I don't want to be indulged to that degree. I'd feel uncomfortable. I'm not used to being plied with things I don't need.'

'What I have in mind will take all the worry out of pregnancy for you.'

'A magic wand?' She laughed bitterly. Raffa didn't join in, and they strolled the rest of the way to the riverbank in silence. When they sat down, Rose took the opportunity to reassure him. 'This isn't your problem. It's mine.'

'There is no problem to solve, there's a child. And this is *our* situation, Rose. You're not alone.'

All the right words, but he sounded so matter-of-fact. You couldn't force someone to love you, no mat-

ter how much you wanted it, Rose reflected as Raffa
went on, 'It makes sense for you to stay here. You'll
have the best of care. Doctors can fly in. You can have
anything, and anyone you want around you. You'll still
be able to work remotely without coming into contact
with the horses.'

'What about my father, and everything else in Ireland?'

'Your father's safe at Sofia's retreat, and I have a
team in place to manage the rest, remember?'

His team. His child. His plan. Rose hugged herself,
wondering about her place in all this, and if Raffa
could ever unbend enough to welcome a baby into
his heart.

CHAPTER FIFTEEN

ROSE SURPRISED HIM by springing up from the river-bank, saying she could do with a rest. His protective instinct kicked in right away. Pregnant women needed lots of rest, he'd heard, though Rose didn't look tired, she looked determined. What was she planning now?

He took her back to the ranch at a steady pace, and saw her safely into the grooms' accommodation with the instruction not to go anywhere near the horses. Mounting his stallion once again, he took a long, fast ride, only slowing when the sun began to dip behind the mountains. The doting uncle—a position he had happily espoused—was destined to become a father. His brother Dante hadn't stopped talking about the wonderful transformation in his life since his wife, Jess, had a child. Could Raffa feel that way too? Did he have the capacity to show a child the love it deserved? And what about Rose? He'd held back from sweeping her into his arms when she'd told him the news because that might have led her to believe that he could be everything she needed when he still wasn't sure himself.

The most important thing now was to persuade Rose to change her mind about accepting his help.

Warp speed described Raffa's reaction to Rose's news. Before the end of the day, Rose had received calls from the secretary of a surgeon-gynaecologist to the royal household in London, as well as from a famous London college where nannies were considered the best in the world. A brief text from Raffa confirmed that he had asked these various individuals to get in touch with her, and that they would be liaising with him once they had spoken to Rose.

And so it begins.

Perhaps he was just being protective, Rose allowed as she waited for Raffa to pick up the phone. Remembering how defensive she'd been when it came to him buying the farm, the pub and the hall back home in Ireland, seeing everything Raffa did as an attempt to control her, she wanted this to be different. It was only natural for him to want the best for his child, and that included looking after the mother. Their baby was all Rose could think about, so she could hardly blame him for that.

'Rose?'

Feeling calmer, she released her vice-like grip on the phone. 'You sound distracted.'

'I'm riding.'

Riding hard, Rose gathered. To get her out of his system? Or maybe to help him come to terms with the news of her pregnancy? 'Can you stop—or rein in, at least? Don't fall off on my account.'

A bark of laughter greeted that remark, followed by a few moments of noisy silence, during which she imagined him reining in and springing to the ground. She waited a beat or two, to give him the chance to get organised, before continuing. 'I've been fielding a lot of phone calls from medical professionals and others.'

'That's down to me,' he confirmed. 'Making sure you have the best care.'

'You know, I could have handled that myself.'

'Let me get back, settle my horse, take a shower, then we'll talk.'

'I'd like that.'

'We'll meet in the yard. Say, half an hour?' he suggested.

She frowned. 'Won't it be dark by then?'

'Full moon tonight. Use plenty of bug spray.'

She wanted to laugh hysterically at his mundane remark, but mostly she fretted that he'd get back safely in the failing light.

There was no fretting when she saw Raffa in the yard…no anger or angst, either, just a wave of deep, overwhelming love. He looked amazing in nothing more than a pair of banged-up jeans and a top that sculpted his freshly showered body. There was a night-blue sweater slung over his shoulders, and his thick black hair was still damp and unruly, as if he hadn't wasted a moment raking it into place before coming to meet her.

'Warm enough?' he asked.

Before she had a chance to answer, he swept the

cashmere sweater from his shoulders and draped it around hers.

'The people I asked to contact you come with cast-iron recommendations,' he explained as they strolled in the moonlight in the direction of the distant pastures. 'The recommendations come from my brother, and his wife, Jess. I wouldn't have suggested these particular professionals otherwise.'

'What's wrong with my family doctor?'

'He's in Ireland.'

'While the specialists you recommend are in London and Madrid?' Rose guessed.

'They're not there now,' Raffa told her with obvious satisfaction. 'They're on their way here as we speak.'

'Don't you think that's a little high-handed?'

He looked puzzled. 'They're the best. They took care of my sister-in-law.'

'And here was me thinking parents decide these things together,' Rose said lightly, not wanting to sour the mood. 'There are two of us involved in this,' she reminded him.

'I don't know what more you want of me, Rose.'

'I don't want you to box off this pregnancy like one of your many projects,' she explained. 'I appreciate you taking the trouble to arrange things, but it would have been much better to discuss it with me first.'

'I've done everything I could think of,' he admitted with a frown. 'I don't understand why you're upset.'

'You're micromanaging me within a few hours of learning I'm pregnant. How did you expect me to feel?'

'That I care about you.'

His words hung in the silence between them. Was she at fault? Was Raffa showing her how much he cared and how keen he was to be a part of this? 'So long as you're not trying to control me.'

'Control you?' He huffed a laugh. 'I stand as much chance of controlling you, Rose Kelly, as I would performing dressage on a wild stallion.'

'But you'd break the horse in eventually…'

He gave this some thought. 'I'd begin by winning his trust, and then I'd train him in the ways I prefer.'

'Wow. Is that what I should expect?'

'And when persuasion failed,' Raffa continued as if he hadn't heard her, 'I'd be forced to think of something else.'

Rose stilled when she saw the look on his face. 'You wouldn't kiss him?' she exclaimed.

'Not like this,' Raffa agreed as he took her in his arms.

What was she doing?

She belonged here.

Why was she kissing him back?

Because there was no other way.

This was hopeless. She was hopeless. How could she resist a man who made her feel as if she had everything to lose and gain in his arms?

Raffa raised a brow when they pulled back briefly. 'But if you'd rather not?'

'I'd rather,' Rose exclaimed, happiness surging inside her. If there were a world of men to choose from, this was the only man she would choose to father her child. Her next and most vital task was to banish the shackles that tied him to the past.

Sex could be wild and fun, or it could be tender and intense. Either way was perfect with Raffa as her lover. His care of her on the riverbank brought tears to her eyes. Release was sweet, complete and draining. But had it changed anything between them? Rose wondered as they lay replete in the sweet-smelling grass. When it came to relieving tension, there was no greater cure than sex, but it didn't always supply a solution.

They walked back to the ranch house together, side by side, but not touching, which led her to wonder, if she wanted things to change, why didn't she do something about it?

They were approaching the grooms' accommodation block when Raffa frowned and asked, 'Why don't you move in with me? It would be so much simpler.'

'For you, or for me?' she asked good-humouredly.

'Everyone on the ranch respects you, and I've come up with the perfect solution to all your concerns.'

'Of course you have,' she teased lightly, loving Raffa for his rock-solid conviction that he was always right, even though it drove her crazy at times.

'Marry me.'

'What?' Rose's mouth fell open. She couldn't have heard him correctly.

'Marry me,' he repeated, as if that were the most obvious statement in the world. 'You trust me. You trust me with your body. You've already admitted that you love me. It can't be such a giant step to agreeing to marry me.'

'Am I expected to take this seriously, or is it another of your jokes?'

'No joke,' he assured her. 'When I think back to my sister's wedding, all I remember is the most bewitching woman I'd ever met putting me firmly in my place. Now that same woman is carrying my baby, and I want to provide for that child—more than provide. I want to see it grow up. I want to teach it to ride, to read, to swim—it's only logical to ask you to marry me.'

'Logical?' Rose interrupted stiffly.

'I won't ask anything of you,' Raffa explained, as if this was what he thought she wanted. 'I'm laying out the most sensible plan.'

'Logical *and* sensible?' Rose's Celtic temper flared. 'Why not add capable to that, while you're at it?'

'Marriage would solve all your problems,' Raffa insisted, as if he had come up with the only possible way forward for them.

Bracing herself, she flashed an angry stare into his eyes. 'I don't have any problems. I'm expecting a baby. Oh, wait. I do have a problem—the baby's father, who speaks every thought in his head without thinking about the hurt he causes.'

'Hurt?' Raffa was clearly taken aback. 'Marriage to me is the perfect solution for you.'

'Because I don't have your means?' Rose challenged. 'I can find a good doctor all by myself, and I'm not afraid of hard work, remember. I was born practical.'

'But you deserve to be loved.'

Everything crumbled inside her. He couldn't have said anything worse. Yes, she deserved to be loved, but he wasn't offering to love her, was he? He was offering a logical solution to her problem. Now she felt like a charity case, with the great Raffa Acosta offering her marriage as a convenient way out. 'I deserve to love too,' she fired back. 'And I will be loved.' As she spoke she instinctively cradled her stomach. Her baby would love her, and she would love it, fiercely.

'You should be thinking about the baby, and what's best for our child.'

'I think about nothing else. I'll provide for our child, and I'll keep you informed—'

'But I love you, Rose.'

She stopped dead. 'What did you say?'

'I love you,' Raffa repeated, meeting her gaze. 'I want to be part of your life. You're the other half of me, the half that completes me. I love you,' he said again. 'My life is empty without you, Rose. If I don't have you to share everything with, it means nothing to me. Wasn't it you who said we're the same? Well, you're right. We're both fighting a past that haunts us—not all at once, we stumble sometimes, and get things wrong, but each time we fall back, you and I, we get up again, and march forward.'

These were the words she'd longed to hear. 'You're serious, aren't you?' she breathed hopefully.

'Never more so,' Raffa assured her fiercely. 'I love you with all my heart, and I'm begging you to be my wife. With you in my life, it will have meaning and love, and hope and dreams for our future. You won't deny me that, will you?'

'You are the most exasperating man,' Rose replied lovingly.

'And you're the most impossible woman on the face of this earth. A good match, I'd say. So, stop asking yourself, can I trust this man? Can I trust what's happening? Those doubts belong in the past. Look forward and know you can trust me, Rose.'

Rose didn't even know why she was crying. This should be the happiest day of her life. When Raffa took her in his arms, *he* knew. 'Did you ever cry for your mother, Rose? Are you thinking right now how much you wish you could tell her your news?'

Her chin shot up. 'How do you know that?'

'I know you. I've taken the time to get to know you, so I understand how well you've learned to hide your feelings, just like I knew, as you know about me, that one day those feelings would have to come out.'

'It isn't easy…'

He huffed a short laugh. 'Don't I know it? *Dios*, Rose, it's such a gift to be able to tell you how much I love you.'

She exhaled shakily. 'You're right.'

'Always,' Raffa teased. 'Your mother would be so proud of you,' he added softly. 'She'll be singing at our wedding.'

That broke the dam. Rose cried, and not in a pretty way. Raffa had unlocked something inside her that she had been unable to do for herself. Longing for things she couldn't have, like her mother's comforting arms around her shoulders one last time—to hear that gentle voice advising her to be strong, almost as if her mother had known what lay ahead. While she sobbed, Raffa held her, and he waited until she was quiet before producing a familiar red bandana from the back pocket of his jeans.

'Better now?' he asked as he mopped her face.

'You won't be able to wear that again.' It was a weak attempt at humour, but it was something.

'I have plenty more,' he reassured her.

Lifting her face to his, she confronted him with what she knew could only be bright, red-ringed eyes. 'And you?' she challenged softly. 'Can you be as open and honest with me as I've been with you?'

Open and honest? Honour was everything to an Acosta, but he knew what Rose was getting at. Giving way to grief was never the easy option. It took strength to reveal sadness and regret as Rose had. Revealing more of himself had been impossible before Rose arrived in his life, because his task had always been to inspire confidence in others. His staff deserved the best of him, and the vast youth following that fame had brought him demanded nothing less.

'You've been as bottled up as I have, but we're both changing for the better, and we'll change faster with a baby coming. If you can't express your feelings, what use are they to anyone?' Rose's question pierced the armour he'd spent a lifetime building, but her next words stripped it clean away. 'I love you completely and utterly, Raffa Acosta. I have since Sofia's wedding when you came out with your outrageous suggestion that we go to bed. I believe you and I have something really special to offer a child, and that's honesty when it comes to feelings and deeds.'

'You're always thinking about other people, Rose. It's time you thought about yourself. I've been heavy-handed in the past, but all I care about is you and this baby. Forgive me?'

'There's nothing to forgive,' she said with the warmth that made Rose so special. 'You blame yourself as I do for things that happened in the past, but could we have done more for our parents? I doubt it. You were a youth, thrilled to be taking them to the airstrip. When that unspeakable tragedy unfolded in front of you, it was bound to leave its mark, but you weren't in a position to instruct your parents what to do, any more than I could stop my father drinking. Hindsight is a great thing, but you can't blame the young man you were, any more than I can be afraid of risking my heart, because I witnessed such a sad version of love at home. We're different people now, you and I.'

'I can't let you be on your own tonight. You're coming with me.'

'Where are you taking me?' she asked as he linked her arm through his.

'To my bed. But not for sex,' he added when she shot him one of her direct looks.

'Not for sex?' she repeated. 'What do you plan instead? A bedtime story?'

The return to the humour they'd always shared was the greatest relief. Cupping Rose's face in his hands, he asked her, 'Do you remember what I said to you that night at the wedding?'

'Every word,' she assured him. 'It isn't every day I'm invited to have sex with a man just to relieve his boredom.'

'Well, now I'm asking you to come to bed with me because I'm madly in love with you, Rose Kelly. I can't live without you. I don't want to try. Give me the chance to hold you in my arms and keep you safe.'

A smile started slowly on her mouth until finally it lit up Rose's eyes. 'And in the morning?' she prompted.

He shrugged and smiled. 'Tomorrow's another day.'

CHAPTER SIXTEEN

ROSE WOKE SLOWLY, unsure for a moment where she was. She only knew as she stretched and rubbed her eyes that she'd enjoyed the best and deepest sleep she could remember.

In Raffa's bed?

She shot up to find him slumbering beside her, spread across every spare inch of the bed. She'd never seen him so relaxed. Running inventory on her sleep-warm body proved they'd slept and nothing more. They'd lifted a huge burden before they'd settled down to sleep together last night. Grief wasn't easily dismissed, but they'd found ways to deal with it. Everything was easier together.

How her mother would have rejoiced at the news of this baby, Rose reflected as she reached for her phone. She'd downloaded an app that showed a child in various stages of development in the womb. Theirs was the size of a blueberry, soon to become a plum, with a lemon and a grapefruit to follow. A fruit salad of joy, she reflected happily as she rested back on the plump bank of pillows.

'What are you doing?' Raffa grunted sleepily.

'I didn't mean to wake you.'

'What's so urgent you had to use your phone? Do you have a problem, Rose? Is it something I can help with?'

'No. Here. Take a look.' She passed the phone.

'What am I looking at?' Raffa asked, perplexed.

'That's the size of our child,' Rose explained.

'Are you giving birth to a blueberry?'

She laughed with sheer happiness. 'No, to a beautiful child.'

Leaning over to share the moment, she felt a tear on her hand. 'Raffa... So, you have no feelings?' she said gently.

No feelings? Raffa was drowning in them. That it had taken the graphic of a blueberry, showing the approximate size of a baby at around six weeks old, was ridiculous—but true. Wherever his feelings had been hiding, Rose had released them. Having started the process last night, she'd delivered the coup de grâce on the small screen of her phone.

'What have you done?' he whispered, accepting and welcoming the emotion overwhelming him.

'I don't know,' Rose responded in the same gentle tone. 'What have I done?'

A wave of regret hit him. 'I wish my parents were alive to see this.'

'And my mother,' Rose agreed softly.

'Life can be cruel.'

'No,' she argued with a firm shake of her head.

'Life is wonderful. Just when you think you've lost everything, you stumble across something new that lifts you to the sky and makes you see the possibilities.'

'You see the bright side of everything,' Raffa commented huskily.

'Not always,' she reminded him. 'I see what there is to be seen. You can see it too. We owe this child of ours to be open and happy, and free from guilt. Let's not burden the next generation with our regret.'

'How did I get to be so lucky?' Raffa growled.

'You asked the wrong woman to go to bed with you?' Rose suggested.

'I asked the right woman,' he insisted. 'I just didn't know it at the time.'

'I only know that I love you, and I understand you, Raffa, and I'll spend the rest of my life proving that you're not to blame for anything, if I have to. When grief and guilt is so deep-seated, it takes time to ease, but we'll keep chipping away until it gets better. I'll always be here for you.'

'Whether I want you or not?' he said.

'Quick study,' Rose approved. 'Even if you send me packing, I'm on the end of a phone.'

'I won't be calling, because you'll be here at my side. I love you with all my unworthy heart. Maybe I should have started with a marriage proposal at Sofia's wedding, and saved myself a lot of trouble.'

'You know I wouldn't have said yes,' Rose countered.

Turning her beneath him, Raffa loomed over her. 'As I'm on one knee at the moment, this seems like the perfect moment for you to answer my question. Will you do me the great honour of becoming my wife?'

'This is not the perfect moment,' Rose argued on a laugh. 'You'll have me saying yes for another reason altogether.'

'I'm prepared to risk it—but hurry up, you're stretching my patience.'

'That's not the only thing that's stretching,' Rose observed wickedly.

'Is that a yes?'

'Yes, I'll marry you,' Rose confirmed, feeling as if her entire world had turned in the right direction at last. 'Of course I will. My answer's...*yes*!'

News that Raffa Acosta, the world's most eligible bachelor, was off the market spread like wildfire. Sofia was the first to congratulate Rose, with Rose's friend Adena hot on Sofia's heels. Some of the publicity regarding Raffa's previous reputation was unkind, but Rose brushed it aside, because she knew the man beneath the hype, the man who was so much more than his press suggested.

Raffa made sure they had plenty of private time to build on the deeper connection that was growing between them every day. They understood each other on so many different levels. When it came to sex, which it so often did, Rose remarked that if she hadn't been pregnant, she would have been by the time they got married.

Their wedding was to be held at Raffa's beach house on the beautiful Spanish island of Ibiza, where their guests could bathe in gin-clear water beneath a cloudless sky. Raffa arranged for the Acosta jet to fly everyone over. It would include a mystery guest, he revealed to Rose this morning in bed. 'I love a good mystery,' he teased, 'but I'm not going to discuss it now, when we have so many better things to do—'

'Like…?'

Rose's question was lost in a shriek of laughter as Raffa brought her on top of him. 'I love you,' she whispered later, when they were both lying contented on the bed.

'Not as much as I love you and our child,' Raffa assured her as he moved down the bed to lavish kisses on the gentle curve of her stomach, before moving even further down, to kiss Rose in the way she could never get enough of, no matter how long they spent in bed.

Sofia and Adena were Rose's attendants at the wedding, with Máire in the role of high-spirited matron of honour. 'Never has so much chiffon and lace been put to better use,' Máire declared as she turned this way and that to admire herself in the mirror. 'You don't look too bad, either,' she told Rose, with a cheeky grin.

Rose's gown was a simple sheath of ivory silk that revealed a hint of the curve of her belly. Rose had no intention of hiding the evidence of her pregnancy, any more than she would try to hide the depth of her feelings for Raffa and her friends on this special day.

Those friends shrieked in unison as Raffa strode unannounced into the room.

'You shouldn't be here,' Sofia scolded her brother.

'Rose?' Switching his demanding gaze to Rose, Raffa only had to raise a brow for Rose's senses to sharpen.

'Could you give us a few minutes?' she tactfully asked her friends.

As soon as they'd gone, she held Raffa to account. 'Must I stand here all day with only a robe covering the dress you're not supposed to see?'

'There's an easy solution,' he advised. 'Take it off.'

Reduced to a quivering mass of love and lust, she slipped out of the dress, and managed to hide it from sight beneath the robe she'd been wearing. 'You're overdressed,' she complained as Raffa took her in his arms. 'Not only that, you have the tang of the stable about you. Have you come here straight from riding?'

'I have an important duty to perform.'

'Call that an excuse?' she asked as he unbuttoned his fly and pressed her back against the wall.

'No. I call this an excuse,' he said as he reached into the breast pocket of his shirt, at exactly the same moment as he took her deep.

'Am I supposed to be able to concentrate?' Rose gasped out.

'Enough to recognise there's no room for a velvet jewel box in my breeches,' Raffa groaned out.

'There's no room for much else but this,' Rose remarked on a half moan, half sigh as he twisted his hips skilfully in the way he knew she loved.

Thankfully, by this time, Raffa had put the box down on the dressing table, all the better to concentrate fully on what he'd come to do. Efficient to a fault, he was fast and firm, and soon had Rose gasping out her pleasure just before he found his. When they were both calm again, he reached for the velvet box.

The wedding ring he'd chosen was a perfect circle of diamonds. 'A symbol of our love,' he explained. 'Fiery, constant and unbroken. But, of course, totally impractical for a hands-on woman like you.'

Rose shook her head in bewilderment. 'So...?'

'So, these are our forever rings.'

He delved into his shirt pocket again, producing another velvet case, this one containing two plain matching platinum bands. 'I've changed the insurance policy,' he explained, 'to accommodate your not-so-secret visits to the stable, and I guessed diamonds would get in the way.'

'Diamonds never get in the way,' Rose protested on a laugh.

'You've changed your tune,' Raffa teased.

'I may be practical, but you've taught me never to be ungrateful,' she said, 'and I promise not to take risks. Our child is too important for that. In fact, I in-sist you accompany me on all my visits to the stable.'

'Deal,' Raffa agreed with a breath-stealing look.

Holding up the glorious diamond circlet to the light, so it flashed blue fire from its prisms, Rose smiled her delight as Raffa drew her into his arms. The kiss lasted perhaps longer than it should have done, but no one was battering down the door yet, and some things couldn't wait.

'As you're so pleased with your diamond ring,'

Raffa remarked as he rearranged his breeches, 'I hope you like this one too.'

Rose could only gape with astonishment as she stared at the magnificent diamond ring he was now holding up. 'What's this for?'

'High days and holidays?' he suggested with a shrug.

The huge, flawless emerald-cut diamond on a slim, diamond-studded band was exquisite. 'I can't possibly,' Rose protested.

'Of course you can,' Raffa insisted. 'Part of our deal demands that I spoil you.'

'Why haven't I seen that clause?' Rose demanded with a teasing smile.

'Put it on,' Raffa prompted softly. 'The diamond is one of a kind, just like you.'

'But I'm not flawless,' she pointed out.

'And I am?' he challenged with a sideways look.

'No, thank goodness, you're not,' she agreed as he reached for her. 'Raffa! No! We can't. There isn't time,' she protested.

Putting one tanned finger over her lips, he proved her wrong.

'Don't shave,' she begged afterwards as he gently rasped his stubble across her neck.

'And look like a ruffian on my wedding day?'

'Just don't,' she begged.

Raffa's black eyes stared into hers, and then he lifted Rose's ring hand to kiss her palm. 'Whatever you say, Rose Kelly.'

There was nothing complicated about love, Rose

concluded. When two people were meant to be together, nothing, not even fate, could intervene. She'd place her hand in Raffa's with total confidence when they joined their lives forever.

Rose and her attendants were escorted to the beach by a Spanish guitarist. The tunes he played moved everyone to tears, or maybe the emotion was due to the mystery guest Raffa had included in the ceremony, as he'd promised Rose.

The reunion with her father, who was waiting for Rose on the beach, to walk her down an aisle composed of white rose petals, came as a complete surprise, and almost threw her. Regaining her composure as fast as she could, she was made up by the change in him. His eyes were clear and his bearing was proud, and he was obviously moved to see his only daughter. 'How can I ever thank you?' he began.

'Don't,' she begged in a whisper as she linked her arm through his to bring him close. 'You don't have to thank me for anything. Your recovery is all down to you. You had to want it, and you had to find the strength to make it happen. I'm so proud of you, Dad, and so glad that you're here. It could never be the same without you.'

'D'you mean that, Rose?'

There were tears in her father's eyes. 'I do,' she stated firmly.

Everything took on a new and brighter aspect as everyone stood to greet the bride. Rose was proud of her father, and so very thrilled to have him walk her down the aisle. In a few short words, he'd explained that Raffa had arranged for her brothers to bring him over. Leaving the retreat was a wrench, he explained, as now he was responding positively to therapy, he was able to help others, which was a much healthier focus than thinking about his next drink.

'Just so long as I don't have to leave the retreat, Rose. I've made my home there now. It's somewhere I truly belong.'

'According to Sofia Acosta, you have a job there for life, if you want it.'

'I do want it,' her father confirmed with feeling. 'I love you, Rose. You've made everything possible, and I know I don't deserve you.'

Raffa had made everything possible, Rose thought as she fixed her gaze on the man she loved, standing unshaven beneath a bridal arch lavishly decorated with flowers as delicate as he was strong.

'Happy?' Raffa whispered as her father placed Rose's hand in his.

'Always and forever when you're around,' she pledged with deep love and trust.

EPILOGUE

Four years later

LOOKING BACK ON the last four years, since what had been termed in the press 'the most romantic wedding of the year', Rose wouldn't have changed a single thing. Two gorgeous rosy-cheeked babies later, she had not had one moment of regret for marrying a man it seemed the entire world lusted after.

Family meant everything to him, Raffa said as he lifted three-year-old Ava Grace into her basket saddle, while baby Luke, who had already perfected the knack of making Acosta-style demands, waited impatiently for his turn.

'And it's great news that Máire wants to take on more responsibility for the retreat in Ireland.'

'Now that I have more responsibility in Spain,' Rose agreed as Raffa led the small Shetland pony while Rose walked alongside.

'The good your father is doing, by helping others at the Irish retreat through his own experiences, is re-markable,' Raffa commented with obvious pleasure.

'Just my brothers to sort out now,' Rose confirmed with feeling. The Kelly clan had gained a new notoriety in the press, thanks to their connection with the Acostas. Rose suspected her brothers weren't altogether displeased about that. It had certainly upped their tally of conquests. They were creating havoc amongst the female population everywhere they went.

'They'll come to their senses eventually,' Raffa soothed, reading her mind.

'As you should know,' Rose remarked wryly.

If it hadn't been for Raffa insisting they could make it together far more successfully and enjoyably than they ever could apart, what would have happened to them? Raffa might never have transformed into the most caring husband and father, and she might have become a slave to her work, but now their happiness was infectious. *Let's hope it stretches to my next announcement*, Rose thought.

'Twins?' Raffa exclaimed, pretending shock at the prospect.

'Not man enough to cope?' she teased, knowing full well that Raffa would be besotted by the new arrivals, and the very first to help out.

'I couldn't be happier,' he assured her. 'Anything and everything to do with you brings me more happiness than I could ever have imagined. As well as the best luck,' he added, referencing a recent huge contract for the Acosta tech company, as well as the fact that Raffa had been voted polo player of the year for the third year in succession. 'Or perhaps my luck's due to this,' he added, kissing Rose. 'The more I kiss you...'

'The more babies we make?'

'Well, if you're already pregnant I can't do any more harm now, can I?' he pointed out with a wicked smile.

Raffa stared deep and long into her eyes.

'You're all I'll ever need, Rose Acosta. You're the love of my life, the mother of my children, and I adore you, now and forever.'

* * * * *

*If you couldn't get enough of the latest story
from the notorious Acosta family,*
Forbidden to Her Spanish Boss,
why not read Cesar and Sofia's story in
The Playboy Prince of Scandal?

And don't miss these other Susan Stephens stories!

The Greek's Virgin Temptation
Snowbound with His Forbidden Innocent
A Bride Fit for a Prince?
One Scandalous Christmas Eve

Available now!

WE HOPE YOU ENJOYED
THIS BOOK FROM
⟨H⟩ HARLEQUIN
PRESENTS

Escape to exotic locations where passion knows no bounds.

Welcome to the glamorous lives of royals and billionaires, where passion knows no bounds. Be swept into a world of luxury, wealth and exotic locations.

8 NEW BOOKS AVAILABLE EVERY MONTH!

#3953 HIS MAJESTY'S HIDDEN HEIR
Princesses by Royal Decree
by Lucy Monroe

Prince Konstantin can't forget Emma Carmichael, the woman who vanished after royal pressure forced him to end their relationship. A surprise meeting five years later shocks Konstantin: Emma has a son. Unmistakably *his* son. And now he'll claim them both!

#3954 THE GREEK'S CINDERELLA DEAL
Cinderellas of Convenience
by Carol Marinelli

When tycoon Costa declares he'll hire Mary if she attends a party with him, she's dazed—by his generosity and their outrageous attraction! And as the clock strikes midnight on their deal, Cinderella unravels—in the Greek's bed...

#3955 PREGNANT AFTER ONE FORBIDDEN NIGHT
The Queen's Guard
by Marcella Bell

Innocent royal guard Jenna has never been tempted away from duty. She's never been tempted by a man before! Until her forbidden night with notoriously untamable billionaire Sebastian, which ends with her carrying his baby!

#3956 THE BRIDE HE STOLE FOR CHRISTMAS
by Caitlin Crews

Hours before the woman he can't forget walks down the aisle, Crete steals Timoney back! And now he has the night before Christmas to prove to them both that he won't break her heart all over again...

#3957 BOUND BY HER SHOCKING SECRET
by Abby Green

It takes all of Mia's courage to tell tycoon Daniel about their daughter. Though tragedy tore them apart, he deserves to know he's a father. But accepting his proposal? That will require something far more extraordinary...

#3958 CONFESSIONS OF HIS CHRISTMAS HOUSEKEEPER
by Sharon Kendrick

Stunned when an accident leaves her estranged husband, Giacomo, unable to remember their year-long marriage, Louise becomes his temporary housekeeper. She'll spend Christmas helping him regain his memory. But dare she confess the explosive feelings she still has for him?

#3959 UNWRAPPED BY HER ITALIAN BOSS
Christmas with a Billionaire
by Michelle Smart

After a rocky first impression, innocent Meredith's got a lot to prove to her new billionaire boss, Giovanni! He's trusting her to make his opulent train's maiden voyage a success. Trusting herself around him? That's another challenge entirely...

#3960 THE BILLIONAIRE'S PROPOSITION IN PARIS
Secrets of Billionaire Siblings
by Heidi Rice

By hiring event planner Katherine and inviting her to a lavish Paris ball, Connall plans to find out all he needs to take revenge on her half brother. He's not counting on their ever-building electricity to bring him to his knees!

HPCNMRB1021

SPECIAL EXCERPT FROM

✚ HARLEQUIN

PRESENTS

*After a rocky first impression, innocent Meredith's got
a lot to prove to her new billionaire boss, Giovanni!
He's trusting her to make his opulent train's maiden
voyage a success. Trusting herself around him?
That's another challenge entirely…*

*Read on for a sneak preview of
Michelle Smart's next story for Harlequin Presents,*
Unwrapped by Her Italian Boss.

"I know how important this maiden voyage is, so I'll give it my
best shot."

What choice did Meredith have? Accept the last-minute second-
ment or lose her job. Those were the only choices. If she lost her
job, what would happen to her? She'd be forced to return to England
while she sought another job. Forced to live in the bleak, unhappy
home of her childhood. All the joy and light she'd experienced these
past three years would be gone, and she'd return to gray.

"What role do you play in it all?" she asked into the silence.

He raised a thick black eyebrow.

"Are you part of Cannavaro Travel?" she queried. "Sorry, my
mind went blank when we were introduced."

The other eyebrow rose.

A tiny dart of amusement at his expression—it was definitely
the expression of someone indignantly thinking, *How can you not
know who I am?*—cut through Merry's guilt and anguish. The guilt
came from having spent two months praying for the forthcoming
trip home to be canceled. The anguish came from her having to be
the one to do it, and with just two days' notice. The early Christmas
dinner her sister-in-law had spent weeks and weeks planning had all
been for nothing. The only good thing she had to hold on to was that
she hadn't clobbered an actual guest with the Christmas tree.

Although, judging by the cut of his suit, Cheekbones was on a huge salary and so must be high up in Cannavaro Travel, and all the signs were that he had an ego to match that salary.

She relaxed her chest with an exhale. "Your role?" she asked again.

Dark blue eyes glittered. Tingles laced her spine and spread through her skin.

Cheekbones folded his hands together on the table. "My role…? Think of me as the boss."

His deep, musical accent set more tingles off in her. Crossing her legs, thankful that she'd come to her senses before mouthing off about being forced into a temporary job she'd rather eat fetid fruit than do, Merry made a mark in her notebook. "I report to you?"

"*Sì.*"

"Are you going on the train ride?"

Strong nostrils flared with distaste. "It is no 'train ride,' lady."

"You know what I mean." She laughed. She couldn't help it. Something about his presence unnerved her. Greek-god looks clashing with a glacial demeanor, warmed up again by the sexiest Italian accent she'd ever heard.

"I know what you mean, and *sì*, I will be on the voyage."

Unnerved further by the swoop of her belly at this, she made another nonsense mark in her book before looking back up at him and smiling ruefully. "In that case, I should confess that I didn't catch your name. I'm Merry," she added, so he wouldn't have any excuse to keep addressing her as "lady."

His fingers drummed on the table. "I know your name, lady. I pay attention."

For some unfathomable reason, this tickled her. "Well done. Go to the top of the class. And your name?"

"Giovanni Cannavaro."

All the blood in Merry's head pooled down to her feet in one strong gush.

Don't miss
Unwrapped by Her Italian Boss.
Available November 2021 wherever
Harlequin Presents books and ebooks are sold.

Harlequin.com